Seeds

A.C. Robbins

*…a **Sector Theoretical** production…*

(Sectortheoretical.com)

Acknowledgments

This novella was proofread and edited by Misty Robbins and Brandi Bunch. Thanks very much to both of you.

Cover artwork by A.C. Robbins. Back cover synopsis by Misty Robbins.

For helping me around the white void, I would like to give a very special thanks to my good friend Gavin Acree, my good friend Joshua Ross, and to my awesome wife Misty.

Special Thanks to Cassia and Trish for being who you are to me and for being awesome enough that I could base a character on each of you. Even though we have no common genetics, you're each my sister and I love you both very much.

Special Thanks to my good friend Pastor Lee Armstrong for the many times he's expounded upon the God-designed, spiritual & biological, natural concept of the seed.

Special Thanks to my good friend Mr. David Anderson for giving me the exact encouragement I needed exactly when I needed it, without which I would most likely not have finished writing this novella nor chosen to have begun the work of Sector Theoretical.

This literary work has been published in honor of Mr. Jack Ross (July 1959 – Dec 2009), the father of my very close friend Joshua and a very great man whom I'm honored to have called a friend. Jack was killed in a car accident, along with his son Jackey, during the writing of this book, hence his name having been given to one of the primary protagonists in the story, so as to honor him in the best way I know how: in writing.

Chapter One

I remember…

I was about seven years old. What with pop bands and friends, I was starting to get a little too old for bedtime stories, but Dad still came to my bedside every night. I think he liked having a little girl a lot more than he liked the idea of having a big one. Despite it all, I still loved being his little girl, so I permitted him a story now and again, but I wanted them to be at least a little romantic. I was too grown up for fairy tales.

I remember, it was a rather ordinary night. Dad walked into my room, knelt down beside the bed to tuck me in, and leaned up to kiss my forehead like he did every night. But then he looked over both shoulders, as if to ensure that no one was within hearing distance, and whispered to me, "This is a special night, lass."

"Why?" I whispered back.

"I've a special story to tell you," he said.

"Will you tell me again the story of how you met mom?"

"That's a good one to be sure, but tonight I've a story about a time *before* I met your ma, back in the old country, with your uncle Drostan. 'Least, that's where it starts anyway."

I loved when Dad would talk about "the Old Country," as he

always referred to Scotland, where he'd been born and raised. My parents had moved to Chicago before I was born to start a new life together. They were happy here and fit well into their new surroundings, but it was obvious that Scotland had and would always have a special place in his heart. "God lives in the Highlands," my father had said to me many times.

"On the farm?" I asked. He'd started so many stories from this same place, so my assumption was a logical one.

"Aye," he said with a nod, "up near Golspie, the land of my youth."

"Will you tell me again about the farm?" I exaggerated my interest just a bit for his benefit.

He raised his eyebrows, "What do you want to know?"

"I don't know," I shrugged, "just what it looked like and stuff."

He smiled, "I've told you a thousand times, Trish-"

"Come on, I just wanna get the picture in my head to fit the story. Please?" I batted my eyes subconsciously.

"Alright," he rolled his eyes, pretending as though this wasn't *precisely* what he wanted, to build up the story.

Dad entwined his fingers to crack his knuckles, an age-old daddy ploy for manufacturing anticipation, and then stretched his arms out to demonstrate, as he began brushing words to canvas.

"A beautiful piece of Highland countryside, The Three Farms; it spread out across the hills. To the high side was the McMillan farm. McMillan had mostly cattle, some dairy, some beef. Dros and I used to best one another as to who could get closest to the bull, piss him off, and make it up a tree." He chuckled to himself at the memory. "A stupid game, that.

"On the low side was the Campbell farm. Campbell had some poultry, but not for profit; his business was mostly potatoes. There were a few patches of wild apple trees that grew in groves here and there, sort of scattered about his land. Every summer, they were covered with bright red, crunchy apples. Dros and I used to eat one now and again.

"Campbell's elderly father lived on the property with them. A good old man he was, but a bit off his head. As far as he was concerned, all his son's land was his, and the scattered, wild apple trees were his orchard. The few times he'd *'caught us in his orchard,'* he'd chased us out with stones. Caught our share of nasty wallops from Old Man Campbell." My dad chuckled at the memory and I had a smile too, at the thought of two mischievous boys getting "wallops" from an old man, yet planning on going back for more later.

"And right there," he continued, "nestled between the McMillan Farm and the Campbell Farm, was ours. Our cattle ran with McMillan's most of the time, no fences, understand; all three farms sort of blended together.

"This was back in times when people could trust neighbors to be neighborly. All the same, we'd only had six or seven cattle anyway; Da was a sheep farmer- a *shepherd*, you might say.

"There weren't any fences for the sheep either of course, though that became slightly more a problem. Sheep are dim-witted animals, understand; invite the wolves and coyotes over for dinner, they will." My father rolled his eyes, sharing with me his exasperation for what he always referred to as "the stupidest of all God's creatures."

Dad's eyes defocused off to some other place and time, probably just as much for my benefit as for actual reverie, "From lads of no more than eight or nine, it became mine and my brother's chore to tend the sheep while Da tended to the wheat crop or helped McMillan with his cattle. But sheep are pretty uneventful for the most part, so the lot of our time was spent inventing games or planning pranks. We'd move the sheep from the front pasture to the back, or whatever Da would tell us, and then go back to whatever particular mischief may have been on the agenda for the day."

I saw the glint in my father's eye and knew that we were about to get into uncharted territory. I leaned forward slightly in anticipation. And so my father began his story…

…It was the year before your grandda had passed away. Dros and I were sharing a flat in Dundee at the time, but we left for a year or so to go back up to the farm. You see, we had made a pact between ourselves, as our father lay sick in bed, to stay with him and tend his sheep for as long as he remained with us.

He loved our ma like no man ever loved a woman. And he raised Dros and me to be men; God-fearing men and no mistake, but no fear of nothing else, mind you.

Da loved the land. He'd take Dros and me for strolls around the farm. "Treat the land with respect," he'd say. "And the animals. The sheep, the cattle; they're our livelihood, but God's given us charge over them, and they're to be treated with honor. A lamb may be our next meal or so, but as long as it lives, it should count on you for a gentle hand. And love the trees, lads," he'd say. "Cut 'em down when you have to, but love 'em. The trees, the hills, the ever-growing green, the earth just asking to be tilled; *God's own country*, this."

It was from him that Drostan and I developed our love for the land and all things that live and grow. That's why we took our chores so seriously. Not one tree would fall without our knowing it. Each little lamb that died was important. In fact, this tale starts with one little dead lamb.

It was out one day on the backstretch when Drostan found the poor wee lamb. We knew he had disappeared some time during the night, but it had taken us all morning to find him. We looked him over but couldn't find any mark on him to explain his death.

"Think it was something he ate?" I asked, as Drostan examined his wee, wooly head.

Dros found on its tongue something curious. It was a tiny, wrinkled seed, the size of a quarter maybe.

"Look at this," Drostan exclaimed, holding up the seed. We both examined it closely. For the life of us, we couldn't tell what it was from. True, we were no botanists, but we had each of us seen the seeds of the plants that grew nearby and none of them had the look of this one.

Drostan was the one who decided to plant it.

"Best way to tell is to see for ourselves," he said, pushing dirt over the wrinkled seed. Then we went away, taking the wee lamb with us.

The next day, looking for a few sheep that had wandered off, your uncle and I returned to the back stretch and found the most beautiful little plant just where we had put the seed. Surprised that there was already growth, we began untangling it from the briars, and you'll never believe what happened.

To our amazement, it shot out of the ground as one big stalk, and split into two at the top, each going a different direction into the clouds!"

"*What?*" I interrupted. "I've heard this one before. – *Fe fi fo fum?* I'm too old for fairytales, Dad."

"Oh, no lass. There may be a familiar part now and again, but you've never heard *this* story, that much I can swear to you–"

"Don't swear."

"Oh, right, you're ma'll have my hide." He looked over his shoulder again. "Now, where was I? Oh, right…"

…So the huge stock forked up into the clouds. And your uncle and I looked at each other, smiling with amazement, and he asked what we should do. I thought for a moment and answered, "We should climb it, don't you think?"

"But we don't know what could be at the top…"

"Aye," I answered, "hence the reason we should climb."

After a moment or two of thinking, my brother agreed with me and we began climbing the massive, green stalk.

Of course, maybe it was foolish of us to decide to climb this magic vine so soon after having seen it for the first time; after all, we had no idea what it was. But our sense of adventure had always been as strong as the Highland air can make it, and we would never have forgiven ourselves had we decided not to go up.

As we climbed, we got more and more excited about our adventure, and I saw that we were coming ever closer to the fork at the top of the vine. I then posed the question, "When we get to the top, which side should we take?"

Drostan stopped climbing for a moment to think, before holding out a fist. "Match for it?"

"Aye… Three times?"

"Three times."

"Alright. Who's which? We're both right-handed."

"I'll be the left."

"Aye."

Clinging to a big, green branch with one arm, we matched with the other.

"Bloody *always*," said Drostan after I'd beaten him, paper over rock both times. "I never win at this."

"So, I say we climb the right, and then come back down later and try the left as well."

"Sounds good to me, mate."

So that's what we did. We continued upward and climbed the right branch of the stalk up into the clouds. We climbed and climbed, up through the big, puffy, white cloud. It felt so strange. You see, looking at the ceiling of the world from the ground is one thing, but climbing into the attic, so to speak, now that's another thing entirely.

When Dros and I were lads, and we'd go with Da to the Glen, I remember waiting all morning for the fog to lift off the misty moors so we could see past just a few feet; well that's what *this* was like, climbing up through the clouds, until we eventually came to the end of the vine, *atop* the clouds.

Now mind you, most people don't know this, but the topside of a cloud is different than the bottom; it's still soft and cushiony like the bottom, but you can walk on it like a floor. And this particular cloud spread out upon green, green grass, into a vast, beautiful meadow in the sky.

Your uncle and I stepped out onto the cloud and walked off into the meadow; it was the most beautiful thing I'd ever seen. There were soft hills that rolled off in every direction, ravines, forests, *mountains* in the distance even. This place was so saturated with life that the green of it nearly shone like gold and silver.

My brother and I stood back to catch our breath, overtaken by this magical land we'd found. About that time, a wee fairy flew up and sat on my shoulder."

"Okay, wait, wait, wait," I smiled, interrupting my father's story. "I allowed the beanstalk for the story's sake, but *fairies*? Come on, Dad."

"Well, you believe in *angels*, don't you lass?" he smiled.

"Yeah."

"What's the difference?"

"Angels are from Heaven," I explained. "Fairies are from *fairytales*. I've told you a hundred times; I'm too old for fairytales."

"You're right, I apologize," he said, before continuing his story, with the ever-brightening glint still in his eye. "Well anyway... Your uncle and I stood back to catch our breath, overtaken by this magical land we'd found. About that time, a wee tiny angel flew up and sat on my shoulder-"

"Okay," I laughed, "you can say fairy."

"What?" he smiled. "Oh, can I? Good, good, good..."

...She was a beautiful lass. Just like a wee tiny person, but with wings of course, she just sat there on my shoulder, batting her pretty little eyes at me, as if waiting for me to say something.

"Who are you?" I asked, when I had somewhat gotten over my surprise.

She looked almost surprised at my question. "I'm a fairy, silly. I should be asking who are *you*?"

"Oh, I'm sorry. I'm Branan. And this is my brother Drostan. We're from down below," I pointed down.

"Below?"

"Aye," added Drostan, pointing to the stalk. "Down the vine… You know… Scotland…?"

The wee lass looked from Drostan to the bunch of wide, green leaves stemming from the top of the stalk which sprouted from the cloud, and back to Drostan, folding her arms with a look of something between irritation and disgust. "I'm sure I don't know what you mean, but you must follow me." And she lit off my shoulder, fluttered her pretty little wings, and drifted toward the meadow.

"But where are we going?" we asked in unison.

"I must take you to the Shepherd."

"The shepherd?" I asked.

She stopped and turned around to face us, hovering several feet above the ground. "Who else do you suppose would care for the sheep?"

"Sheep?" we asked in unison again.

She looked back at us, dumbfounded by our ignorance, "The sheep of the Kingdom…"

"What kingdom?" asked Drostan.

At this, her mouth dropped open in shock. "…The sheep live in the Kingdom, the Shepherd who cares for them stands at the gate. He's the only way in to the Kingdom… You two really need to become more educated." She shook her head and turned, fluttering on in the direction she had started. So my brother and I, not knowing what else to do, followed the wee lass through the meadow.

The beautiful, green, pillowy hills seemed to go on and on, and once we'd crested the first hill, we saw that the meadow was nearly *full* of fairies. Their little wings propelled them one direction and the next, each doing her little fairy chores.

Just like little bees, they kept very busy with this and that, though it was never obvious exactly what any of them were doing. My brother and I watched it all, both smiling as we followed our guide, and before we knew it there we were, standing at a large, stone gate.

At the gate, we saw an old man standing, with a staff in one hand about as tall as himself.

"Hello there, little Miss, Miss Glllorrriiiaaa," he stretched her name out uncertainly, as if attempting to remember it as he spoke.

His voice sounded like that of an old man, and he looked it enough: old robes, long, gray beard; but somehow, his eyes made him look young.

"Charity, my lord, Miss Charity."

"Oh yes, yes, I'm sorry. There are just so many of you, you know. What have you got?"

"Requesting entry, my lord," said our guide. Really, Drostan and I had to smile. It was so funny to see something that tiny being so self-important. As we tried not to laugh, I suddenly caught the eye of the old man, the Shepherd as he was supposedly called. It seemed as if he knew exactly what was on my mind and, if the smile in his vibrant eyes was any indication, he found her mannerisms very amusing also.

"I found these two in the meadow," little Miss Charity continued. "They're from a place called Spot Land."

"Actually, Miss- uh- Charity," I interrupted as politely as I knew how, "technically, it's *Scot*land."

"All the same," she continued, slightly irritated, "they're from outside the meadow, so I brought them to you. Now, if I may have leave, my lord, I have many chores." The Shepherd nodded, and Charity fluttered away.

There was a long, awkward moment of silence as my brother and I stood there looking at the Shepherd, waiting for him to speak. Realizing the Shepherd's apparent contentment with the awkward silence, Drostan decided to be the one to break it.

"So we found this fat little seed, and we planted it, and it grew up into the sky; and I'm sorry if we shouldn't have climbed it, but-"

"Curiosity got the better of us, I suppose," I interrupted.

"Aye, and so we climbed up into the clouds and came out into this meadow, and that's where we met Miss Charity."

The Shepherd smiled a smile that made me feel good inside, and then finally spoke, "You may enter the Kingdom. I ask of you only one favor at this time: that you find for me a particular precious jewel. I have seen it not for some time, and I long to have it back."

And then he reached into a pouch which hung from a long strap around his shoulder and pulled out two little seeds, much like the one we'd seen in the wee lamb's mouth.

"A seed for you each," he said with a smile. "Treat it wisely." And then he moved aside to let us through the gate. After an unsure glance to each other, we thanked the Shepherd and accepted the seeds.

Passing through the gate, we stood at an elevated place that overlooked the Kingdom. Our mouths dropped open in awe, as we looked out over a city that seemed to go on forever in every direction, like in the fairy tales. It was the perfect marriage of all that which grows and stone. A great, white stone city it was, nearly covered in moss and ivy, grass and trees.

People went from one place to another, apparently busy with whatever they were doing. Some were obviously shop owners, talking up their fare, be it bread or leather or stone or plant. Others went about from store to store getting whatever it was they had need of for the day. Each looked lost in his own little world. The quaint beauty of the city, mixed with the vibrant life created by the bustle of the people, left Drostan and I shocked over the magic of it all.

"It's the most beautiful thing I've ever seen," whispered Drostan.

"Aye."

We stood in silence, merely taking it in.

"You think they've got a football team?" Drostan finally said with a satirical grin.

"Aye," I smiled back, "I saw them at Ibrox last season. Lost by one goal."

"Aye," he laughed, "good game, that one."

We followed the little pathway down the grassy, green slope, which opened up into the city. The pathway, which became a stone avenue, ran down the center of the city for miles, the main street from which all the others stemmed, as far as you could see.

We smelled the gorgeous aroma of freshly baked sweets wafting from little pastry shops. We heard the brewing of hot coffees and the ching of wineglasses and fine silver as we walked by several scattered sidewalk cafés. We saw enormous libraries looming here and there in all the pomp and state of historical memorandum.

There were blacksmith shops with hot irons glowing, glass shops with mirrors reflecting the sun, art supply shops with paints lining the walls. There were so many shops and alleyways that we couldn't even count, and people were swarming everywhere.

They looked, in apparel and demeanor, as though from a time past, not all that dissimilar from the Shepherd. We nodded to those who paid us notice as we passed, just to be cordial like.

After a few blocks, we remembered the promise we'd made.

"We can't forget the lost jewel," Drostan said, just before stopping a big, strong looking man who carried with him a strangely shaped hammer.

"Excuse me, Sir," he began, "you wouldn't know anything about a lost jewel, would you?"

"No, I'm sorry, I don't," said the large man with a friendly smile that didn't quite match his gruff voice.

"I'm Branan," I said, extending my hand to his, "and this is my brother Drostan, and we're sorry to bother you, but we're from outside the Kingdom-"

"Well then," he interrupted with a handshake that was almost violent in its enthusiasm, "allow me to introduce myself lads! Name's Gunty, and as you can see, I'm a stone-crafter."

"Actually, I d-"

"I and my kind have fashioned the stone surfaces of the Kingdom for near twenty years now. And before me, others like me, my ancestors in fact, did just the same." He was much honored to have the profession he did, we could tell.

"Well, it looks to me as though you do a rather good-"

"There's always a need for shapin', reshapin', fashionin', refashionin'; it never stops. That's why the Kingdom always looks brand new. Why, I remember when I was just a lad-"

"Gunty!" called a voice from somewhere about half a block away.

As Gunty turned to see who was calling his name, the voice rang out again. "Gunty! Is that you? There's aye a pillar in the courtyard needs a chisel, as you well know," called the man, as he walked up to us with a woman beside him, "and the same awaits you now. Thought you might appreciate the opportunity."

"Aye Thomas, I thank ye!" And off he went with pride in his work and hammer in hand.

"Lads," greeted the man as he reached out his hand once Gunty was out of sight. "I'm Thomas, and this is my wife Penny; tailor and seamstress, at your service. We've a shop just a wee stroll from here, by the way… I do hope the conversation we interrupted was of little importance."

"What- oh, it's alright," I said.

"It's just that," added Penny, "well, if you don't mind our saying so, we could tell by your dress that you're foreigners, and well, we wanted to spare your ears."

"What do you mean?" asked Drostan.

"Well," continued Thomas, "it's just, I mean, no *disrespect* to the mates, understand, but those stone-crafters are more proud of their job than anyone should take the effort to be. Talk your ears off they will."

"How long have you been?" interjected Penny, before we'd really had time to process exactly what we'd heard. "Here in the Kingdom, I mean. Have you planted any seeds yet?"

"Seeds?" we asked in unison.

"It's easy to go and just keep going," Thomas chimed in, "but just a word to the wise: if you have any, be sure and pay them notice. They're a beautiful thing, seeds."

With a smile and glance to her husband, Penny commented, "I remember the seeds that brought us together."

"Aye," he answered with a wink, "cotton."

"Indeed. Found ourselves planting in the same fields…" Penny trailed off, as she seemed to get lost in her husband's eyes.

"…Romantic," Drostan said awkwardly in a tone that only I could tell was sarcastic. But what else could be said? Neither he nor I had any idea what they were talking about.

"Well, we better be going," I said, before they could begin talking again. "It was a pleasure to meet you, but we've got a task at hand."

"Don't suppose you'd know where to look for a precious jewel?" Drostan threw in, almost as an afterthought.

"Aye, three blocks and to the left," Thomas pointed. "Nicolai the Jeweler has a shop just a jaunt up Ivy Road. I'm sure he can help you find what you're looking for." At this, the four of us exchanged parting pleasantries and went our separate ways.

Chapter Two

We found the jeweler's shop without too much a problem. The sign read: *Ivy Road Gems*. A man whom I assumed to be Nicolai stepped in behind the counter from somewhere in back, and it hit me at once that he fit the prospect of a jeweler, or at least my idea of it, as I'd never known a proper jeweler.

He was very sleek in dress, though ironically, his eyes showed him to be a trustworthy man. He introduced himself, and I asked him where we might find a precious jewel. He showed us several of his most gorgeous pieces, until I realized we had a misunderstanding.

"-I'm sorry to interrupt, brother," I said, trying to be polite, "but I believe I've given you the wrong impression. These are all very nice pieces to be sure, but we've not come here to buy, we're looking for a precious jewel that's been *lost*."

"Oh... No worry, lads," he assured us. "But if you're looking for a *lost* jewel, then you're looking in the wrong place. Nothing's lost in the Kingdom, everything has been found, that's why it's *in* the Kingdom in the first place."

Aye, right. What was that supposed to mean? A glance from Drostan showed me that he was equally stupefied, so we thanked Nicolai for his help, and were on our way. As we left the shop, Nicolai called out, "And good luck with your seeds."

As we continued down the street, I pondered this last statement, and my brother presented the exact question that had been on my mind.

"What's the deal with *seeds*?"

"Exactly," I answered, "I'm wondering the same thing. Suppose they've got some sort of value to these people?"

"-I should bloody think so," he interrupted with a smirk, "I mean, they keep talking about how pure dead great it is just to find one, no?"

"Aye," I laughed, "But I mean, you think it's like, a form of money to them?"

"I don't think so. I saw tickets in the jeweler's shop. It was all pounds."

At this, we both looked up to see that we were now standing at the street-side counter of another little shop. Looking over the counter, I saw that the shop was almost exactly evenly divided down the middle. On one side were rubber chickens, balloons, whistles, wax teeth, funny glasses; on the other side were sparklers, poppers, screamers, fire-crackers, and the like. Looking up above the counter, I read a sign engraved in funny letters: ***Baggs' and Gains' Gags and Bangs.***

"Donald Baggs," said a man with a big smile, popping his head up from behind the counter and jutting out his hand in greeting. He was dressed in a striped suit that was quite laughable, which I assumed was *indeed* the point.

"And I'm Willard Gains," said a second man, popping up beside the first and jutting out his hand as well, dressed nearly the same.

We shook their hands, glancing to each other in agreed acknowledgment of their trite silliness.

"What's your celebration?" asked the first, smiling over-excitedly, eagerly awaiting my brother's answer.

"...Actually, we're just passing through..."

"Well then, we hope you enjoy your journey," said the other to me. "At least take a few fire-crackers, at no cost," he smiled, putting a matchbook and a wad of blackjacks in the hand he'd finally finished shaking.

"Um, thanks," I said, stuffing them in my pocket.

"Good day to you gentlemen," they said, smiling and waving as we began to walk away.

"And the same," we waved.

After we'd reached a distance out of earshot, Drostan said rather quietly, "That was *awkward*; almost frightening even."

"Aye," I laughed, "a bit. They seem like nice enough lads though."

"As are circus clowns, but I don't intend to converse with them."

After walking for just a few moments, there was another little shop that caught my eye, at least enough to warrant stopping for a moment. It looked almost like a little open greenhouse. There were jars and cans here and there with wee plants growing out the tops, along with different growing specimens of this or that scattered about.

Above the front counter read the name: **Jaron the Planter**, under which read: *find a home for your seeds*.

"Find a home for your seeds, lads?" We looked down to the counter to see a man standing behind it with a smile.

Pointing to the sign, I asked, "Jaron?"

"The very same," began his sales pitch. "And for a small fee, I'll accept any excess seed, regardless of size or potential, and find a good place for it to flourish."

"Ahhg," said Drostan under his breath, "here it goes again..."

"How goes it mate?" I jumped in, reaching out my hand to his. "We're from a place called Scotland; do you know it?"

"Where?" he smiled, with a look that showed almost childish bewilderment.

"Nevermind," I continued, still smiling. "We're outsiders; our first visit to the Kingdom, understand, and we can't seem to find our way around this *seed* thing."

"Aye," chimed in Drostan, "What's the big deal with seeds? I mean, of course, there are seeds in Scotland as well, but... It's not like..." He trailed off.

"Here in the Kingdom," explained Jaron with a smile, "everyone is given at least one seed. The only stipulation to seeds is that you have to plant each one and give it space to flourish." Then Jaron's tone became slightly more dramatic, "Any seeds hoarded up and kept will go sour."

"So big deal," said Drostan with a shrug. "Why does that matter?"

Jaron suddenly became very serious. "Beware the Dragon. The Dragon is drawn to unused seeds. He seeks them out and will nest where they may be found, making that place his lair. Any *good* which may otherwise have come from the seed will be replaced with evil."

Drostan and I exchanged glances. What was this? I wondered. This strange place seemed to grow stranger by the second.

"…Aye, right," said Drostan, sort of rolling his eyes.

Seeing that my brother was beginning to come off a bit rude, I pretended to act interested. "A real dragon?"

"Indeed," answered Jaron, turning his attention to me.

"And it's ever about the Kingdom?"

"But a breath away, he is, aye waiting to pounce," he said, almost fearfully.

"Aye, right. So prepare us," said Drostan in mock seriousness, "what's this dragon look like?"

Jaron's eyes looked away, "Well, to be sure, I've never actually seen him."

"Pure dead shocker-" mumbled Drostan just before I caught him in the shoulder with an elbow.

"We appreciate the warning, sir," I said outright loud to drown out my brother's rude comment. "We'll be on our guard." And we were on our way.

All along the stone avenue, there had seemed quite a healthy bit of commerce, but only now, continuing on our way, had we come to what appeared to be *the busy section*, as it were.

These shops seemed almost as if they were stacked, one upon another. And the people may as well have been stacked just the same, buyers and sellers shouting one to another, trying to hear over the noise of the bustle to conduct their respective business.

And of course in this stretch there were also more cafés, pastry shops, and the like, so as to exploit the bustle.

Eventually giving in to the alluring smell, we stopped at a fine pastry shop, supposing it couldn't hurt to sit for a pastry or two. The host of the shop was a man named Jonathan. He greeted us and we made conversation at a peaceful table over a couple strawberry pastries and a cup of coffee apiece.

"Nice place," my brother said, looking around the shop appreciatively, and I truly believed he meant it.

"Aye, I thank ye," said Jonathan.

He told us how he'd gotten his start, mentioning that, "thanks to a seed he'd found when he was just a lad, he had the ability to make fine pastries."

"What's a seed have to do with pastries?" I asked.

"Well, once I was of age," he explained, "I wanted to run my own shop. The seed I had planted as a lad had grown to be a beautiful vine of big, plump grapes. It was a respectable plant, understand, but it served little purpose to my dream of being a baker, so I was discouraged and began to question my dreams and ambitions.

"But then I remembered that my best friend as a lad, Jonas had always wanted to run his own winery, so I gave Jonas my grapevine.

"I felt good inside, helping Jonas to achieve his dream, but was still sad that I was no closer to achieving my own. Shortly after, Jonas informed me that the first seed he ever found as a boy had since grown to a respectable patch of sugarcane. He had no use for it, and said I could have it."

"That was nice of him n'all," thought Drostan aloud, "but I'm assuming the sugarcane doesn't sprout pastries, so how does that help you?"

"I still have to *make* the pastries. Which incidentally gives me the freedom to be as creative with flavors and textures as I fancy, but as everyone knows, a good pastry is a sweet pastry, and I have all the sugar I'll ever need growing out back."

I looked out back where he aimed his thumb, and then back to him, "So by giving away what you had, you ended up with what you wanted, no?"

"Aye," said Jonathan, "and more. The patch of sugarcane is adjacent to a small coffee field owned by a woman named Sarah." He pointed again to the growth behind his shop. "She helps me harvest the sugarcane, I help her harvest the beans-"

"-And you have a coffee shop right next door to your pastry shop," I interjected, pointing my thumb to the coffee shop to the left of us.

"Everybody likes coffee with their pastries, no?" smiled Jonathan, proud of himself for having conceived such an idea in the first place.

"Indeed," agreed my brother, lifting his cup to his mouth.

As I looked in the direction of my thumb, I saw, to my surprise, not far away from the coffee shop counter the Shepherd walking with his staff.

"I thought the Shepherd stayed at the gate...?" I queried aloud, turning back to Jonathan.

I noticed Jonathan's expression had changed from cordiality to suspicion, as he looked over my shoulder into the street at the subject of my question. "That's not the Shepherd of the Gate," he said, in a strange, somber tone.

My brother and I both turned again to look. It certainly *appeared* to be the Shepherd.

"Would either of you like some more coffee?" he asked, changing the subject as quickly as possible. "I can have Sarah serve you each another cup at no cost to you."

At this, combined with having just seen a shepherd of some sort, I realized that though these Kingdom people were good people, they seemed to be helping us waste our time; we didn't have time for coffee. We had a promise to keep to the Shepherd, and the longer we sat in shops being comfortable, the less time we spent looking for the Shepherd's jewel.

"We do appreciate the hospitality, brother," I said as cordially as I knew how, "and we've both enjoyed your fine pastries, haven't we Dros?"

"Better than any in the whole of Scotland," interjected my brother, finishing the last of his strawberry streusel and licking his fingers.

"But we must be going," I continued, as my brother and I got up from the table, backing toward the street. "We've a promise to keep and a jewel to find, understand."

"Alright then," answered Jonathan, in a passively offended disposition, to which I shrugged apologetically.

Drostan and I turned about and found ourselves facing a wall of people in the street. We joined the stream and began walking in the direction we assumed the shepherd had gone.

We walked for longer than I'd assumed we'd have to.

After several minutes, we both stopped in the middle of the street, scratching our heads. The shepherd we'd seen only moments earlier was nowhere to be found. We looked up and down the street, but it was like he'd just disappeared.

Fearing we'd clog up the street, we just kept moving. Asking person after person, it seemed no one else had seen him, and I wondered if somehow our eyes had played tricks on us.

"*You* saw a shepherd in the street, right?"

"Aye," answered Drostan. "The baker saw him as well."

"Strange," I thought aloud, looking in all directions, "I wonder where he's gone..."

"...So what now?"

"Mmm...?" I shrugged.

He thought for a moment, "Do you suppose we should leave the Kingdom?"

"What? Why would we need to leave?"

"I'm just saying," he added, "we're looking for a lost jewel. If nothing's lost in the Kingdom, like the jeweler said, then it stands to reason-"

"That we're going to have to leave to find it," I finished his sentence, realizing the validity of this statement.

"Aye. Maybe we should try the other branch of the vine..."

In my enjoyment of the wonders of this Kingdom, I had forgotten all about that second branch.

"I suppose you're right. But," I added, my heart sinking, "I'd rather not have to backtrack all the way to the meadow though. And we've got all the time in the world as far as we know. Let's stay on the street for awhile, see where it takes us."

My brother agreed with me, and so that's what we did.

Eventually, after what seemed like hours of aimless walking, we came to what looked like the end of the street. Everything at this end of the avenue was less cared for it seemed, as if this were part of the Kingdom that everyone avoided.

"What's this, mate?" said Drostan, as he pointed toward a small, street-side shop just a few strides from us.

Walking towards the ragged little shop, we saw that it was set up much like most of the other shops we'd already seen: a counter and a sign above it.

The place was a proper rubbish heap, tattered canvas like a

sagging umbrella hanging over the sides from the top, many of the boards crooked or falling off from missing fasteners. It may as well have had a "*Go Away*" sign.

"The Viner," Drostan read the sign aloud.

"That's strange," I added. "There's no name. Like *Jaron* the Planter, *Jonathan's* Pastry Shop, *Sarah's* Coffee Café... It just *The Viner*..."

"The *Viner*," Drostan said again, before sharing with me his revelation, "maybe they know a shortcut to the vine in the meadow."

I was still dubious, "The sign says *The Viner*, Dros; not *The Random Unexplained Magical Viner*."

Drostan shrugged off my doubt as if it were nothing, "As if any of the rest of this Kingdom makes sense- It's worth a go, mate."

I shrugged and we went forward.

Stopping just at the counter, there was an unsure look to each other, as no one was there. Drostan shrugged, and then knocked at the counter.

To our obvious surprise, out from the back quarters of the shop came the shepherd we'd seen in the street earlier.

"Good afternoon, gentlemen," he said. "What can I do for you?"

"Um," I stammered a bit, "We were actually looking for you, Sir."

"For me?" he smiled. "And why is that?"

"We saw you in the street a ways back," chimed in Drostan.

"We thought you might be someone else at first."

"The Shepherd of the Gate?"

"Aye," we agreed.

"No harm; common mistake. So many people make that assumption of me; as if he were the *only* shepherd," he smiled. "Where are you lads from?"

"We're from outside the-" Drostan stopped himself, "That's funny you should ask. Most people here, until we've pointed out otherwise, have just assumed that-"

"With my age comes wisdom; I can see that you two have a bit too much wit to truly belong here among these poor dim-witted sheep."

"What do you mean?" I asked.

"Understand; I mean no offense to this beautiful Kingdom, but sheep aren't so named for nothing," he smiled.

Drostan and I grinned to each other, still not quite understanding why he was calling them sheep, but having seen enough of the strange people for me to add, "The same offense not intended, but we totally understand..." The three of us exchanged knowing smiles.

"So what brings you to my shop, lads? Well, aside from following me here..." We laughed.

"Well, to be honest with you," answered Drostan, "we're looking for a way out of the Kingdom."

"That bad, is it?" he said with a small chuckle.

"No, I- I don't mean it like that," smiled Drostan. "We plan to come back; we just need to leave for awhile."

"Which way do you plan to take?"

"Once again," I chimed in with a smile, "it's funny you should ask. We had planned on going back through the Kingdom to the meadow, and maybe trying the other branch of the vine."

"Going back?" his smile made me feel naïve. "No sense in going all the way back to the meadow. Sure, the Shepherd of the Gate might want you to believe there's only one way-"

Odd. The Shepherd hadn't said anything about that.

"Well, he never actually-"

"But there's more than one way to do just about anything," he continued, ignoring what I was saying. "I can offer you an easier way. Follow me." He opened the little door to the side of the counter and welcomed us in.

My brother and I sort of shrugged to each other, which seemed to be becoming a custom of late, and followed the shepherd to the back quarters of the shop.

It looked like the back quarters of any shop, I suppose. There were several tools scattered about, and shelves with various items stacked and whatnot. But unique to this room was a large hole in the floor, around which everything else was oriented.

There, we saw a thick, green vine, just like the one in the meadow. It stood up about waist high from the hole.

"I believe this is what you're looking for, gentlemen. This will take you to the fork in the vine."

"Wow," we said in unison. "Thank you, sir."

"My pleasure, lads," he said with a wink. "Should you need anything else, you know where to find me."

And so, after exchanging pleasantries, my brother and I climbed down through the hole in the floor and descended the magical vine through the clouds.

Chapter Three

So your uncle Drostan and I climbed up the *left* branch of the stalk and into the clouds. Atop these clouds was very much the same as before, soft and cushiony and yet firm enough to stand on.

This time however, instead of opening out into a meadow, we found ourselves staring at the wall of an old building.

"I don't know why," began Drostan, "but something about this place feels creepy."

"Aye, agreed. We should play it safe, no?"

"Aye."

We crept around, trying to stay out of sight until we found a window we could climb in through.

"Should we climb in?" I asked.

My brother, always a bit more one to dive into uncertainties, shot me a questioning brow, "It's what we came for, isn't it?"

"Aye, but I'm thinking; did you trust that shepherd?"

He sort of shrugged, "Didn't really think about it, I guess. He did help us find exactly what we were looking for, brother..."

"Aye, but... something bothered me about him. I couldn't put my finger on it, but it's like... well, you know how the Shepherd of the Gate looked like an elderly gentleman, except his eyes were younger like, friendly. That's a strange combination, to be sure, but somehow it was calming."

"Agreed. What's your point?"

"Well, this other shepherd was like, backwards. He looked young, even in the face, but his eyes were ancient, cunning, very serpentine, if you take my meaning."

Drostan laughed at my serious attitude, "I think you're reading a bit much into this, pal."

"...Maybe," I admitted, dropping the subject, as Drostan reached up to prop open the window.

Once on the inside, we found ourselves in a sort of mop closet. Creaking open the door a bit to peek out, we saw a long white corridor. Seeing no one in either direction, I figured it might be safe to venture out.

"Let's go," I whispered to Drostan. I took one more look to be sure then stepped out, with Drostan right behind.

My heart jumped; no sooner did we shut the door to the mop closet behind us than appeared five people in white coats, three men and two women standing but a few inches from us.

"Welcome, welcome, welcome!" said the five in unison.

"Bloody hell," breathed Drostan, quite taken aback.

"Welcome to Seed Incorporated," continued the man in front, who looked strangely familiar, as the other four smiled with him.

"All that's required is a little faith in the product we provide," said one of the men behind.

"-hope for a providential future by means of our product," continued the man on the opposite side.

"-and our product itself," continued the two women in unison, before all four continued in unison, "-The Seed."

Without missing a beat, the man in front continued, "Tour of the factory, gentlemen?"

Then it hit me: the man in front was the shepherd we'd just spoken to, or appeared to be by all accounts. His hair was different and his clothes were different, but staring back at me were those same snake eyes I couldn't trust.

"Shepherd...?" I asked, not knowing how else to address him.

"Excuse me?" he replied, politely smiling and raising his eyebrows.

"Aren't you... we just...?"

The curt smile that was his only reply acknowledged absolutely nothing, but his eyes I still couldn't trust.

"Follow me," he said.

The five white coats turned in unison and marched down the corridor, not even looking to see if we were coming, so we sort of shrugged to each other and followed.

I still didn't completely trust the shepherd, or his odd workers, but I was curious to see where we were.

Our first turn stepped us through a doorway, crowding the seven of us onto a little balcony that overlooked a huge room full of artificial sunlight and people bustling over all kinds of plants.

"We call this room The Greenhouse," said the lead man, as all five tour-guides watched us, smiling. "This is where we produce all the seed-bearing plants. -Right this way," he said, as he continued on.

We followed back out into the corridor and down it until we came to another open doorway, this one on the opposite side, and stepped through it. We saw a laboratory of some kind, with many pieces of what looked like highly technical equipment sitting, standing, and hanging about, all of which seemed to be in use. Several scientists looked up, paying our group a brief moment's notice, and then continuing with their research.

"This is engineering," said our guide. "Every seed contains natural elements of fulfillment corresponding to the seed's natural potential. Our engineered enhancements to said elements make the seeds we produce all the more desirable. One more way of staying ahead of the competition," he said with a smile, as the five simultaneously winked in implication.

As we exited the lab to reenter the corridor, Drostan leaned over to me, "These people seem a bit creepy to you?"

"Aye, something's wrong about this whole place, I think."

"Agreed," he replied, as we stepped through a new doorway.

"This is our Promotions Department," continued the tour-guide, interrupting our whispered conversation. "As desirable as we've engineered the seeds to be, it is of no consequence until the target demographic takes the proverbial bait, if you will. Marketing is key. To *convince* an individual that our product is a *necessity* is the first step to retaining a repeat customer."

He stared at us as if expecting some sort of answer, so I nodded my head. He seemed pleased with that and turned to leave.

Moving along, we followed our guides through yet another doorway, this room similar in size and appearance to the first. The hands of the staff moved busily, as hundreds, possibly thousands of boxes were filled, sealed, moved along rollers and conveyors, and shipped out on motorized dollies.

"As you no doubt have guessed," said our host, "this is Outgoing. These are the hands that meet our customers' needs." He watched the day's production with pleasure, looking out over the thousands of neatly packaged seeds. He lifted two fingers to his brow in a salute of affirmation to the floor manager below, and once it was returned, did an about face, leading us out the doorway.

"That concludes our tour gentlemen," he said, after we'd entered a vaulted, sterile-white lobby, lined at the front with crystal-clear, glass doors. "We hope you've enjoyed your visit," and then we were gently, "politely" pushed out the glass doors, which were locked behind us.

We stood staring for a moment in confusion. What had all that been about?

Standing on the sidewalk in front of the factory, Drostan and I looked around ourselves to find that we were in a town, or *city* more like. Unlike the clean, sterile inside of the factory, the city surrounding it seemed to be immensely polluted and poverty stricken. At the side of the street, between the factory and the city, was a sign.

"Welcome to Exploit," I read aloud with a dry laugh. "Sounds like the start of a bad joke."

"Strange enough name for a city anyway," reflected Drostan.

I looked around us at the cracked, hole-strewn streets and the tall buildings, standing in bad repair, as if they would collapse at any moment, "Doesn't seem to be a very happy town…"

"Suppose *they've* got a football team?" he asked with half a smile.

"I don't suppose they've got a bloody *football*, much less a team. This place looks worse than London. I'd suppose it's like in the gangster films; where like two or three rich men own everything and no one else can even afford a pint."

"Not even a pint? What a miserable world that would be-"

"I'm being serious," I shunned his joke. "This is a bad place. Assuming there are people here; they're probably in a miserable state."

"What, like Texas?"

Shaking my head in disgust, I ignored his cold sense of humor, moving toward an alley between two large buildings as he finished his joke, mostly to amuse himself, "At least, according to what I've read; with all the *sagebrush*, or whatever it's called, and those big, silly hats…"

Walking down the alley, we heard a loud squawk from above. We both cocked our heads back to look up, and saw probably the biggest bird I'd ever seen, even to this day, perched on the ledge of a jagged roof. He was staring at us, right at us both, as if he was going to say something.

"That's a bird?!"

"Looks like," I mumbled, still staring into the bird's big, dark eyes.

"He's flipping huge-"

"You gentlemen new here?" he interrupted in a deep, curt, intelligent voice.

My brother and I jumped a bit, blatantly apprehensive about being addressed by a falcon. "We're sort of... visiting," I answered.

"Not by choice?"

"Not... exactly," answered Drostan.

"I'm Hawk," he continued, after a moment's silence. "If you ever need me, just call." And then he squawked loudly, stretching out his enormous wings and flying away into the distance.

After a heavy moment of silence, both staring off in the direction Hawk had flown, my brother and I attempted to snap out of the awe of the situation.

"Certainly a first for me," said Drostan. "You?"

"I wonder what he is," I thought aloud.

"As far as I can tell, he's a giant talking bird named *Hawk*."

"Shut up, you know what I mean. I mean, I wonder where he came from, or what his *purpose* is here, no?"

"Don't forget, brother," began Drostan, with a hand on my shoulder, "we got here by climbing a huge magical vine into the clouds."

"Point taken."

At this, we heard a noise from somewhere in the alley behind us.

"Eh boys-"

Drostan and I turned to see a woman standing, holding something in her hand. I looked at her, sort of assessing the situation. The woman looked as though she was probably very pretty at one time, but was now nearly skin-and-bones, like she was dying from the inside out. It made me feel sad.

As I looked closer, starting at her hand, I saw that what she had was a little handful of seeds. They were dried up, with very little look of life yet in them. Following my eyes up her arm, I saw a web of light blue veins through her nearly translucent, taut, unhealthy skin.

Her tattered rag of a shirt hung off one shoulder, crossing her bony body at an angle that barely covered her chest. Her hair and makeup were an obvious attempt for male attraction, over-utilizing what little composure she had left.

She winked at us with a smile, "Out-of-towners, yeah? Do you beautiful men want some seeds? Give you a good price, guaranteed."

Drostan, suddenly very serious, gave me a side-long glance and whispered, "Is this what I think it is?"

"Certainly appears to be."

We both just sort of stood there looking her direction, trying to decide what to do.

"This is definitely not the type of woman I would normally suggest we associate with," he whispered, "but I think we should talk to her. For *her* sake if nothing else."

"Agreed," I reciprocated.

So my brother and I put on our best smiles and tried not to act awkward.

"What's your name, lass?" asked Drostan.

"I'm Crystal, guv. You?" she winked again; slowly, subconsciously sliding her hand in a soft caress down her side.

"I'm Drostan and this is my brother Branan. What's this?" he nodded to her open hand.

"Like I was saying," she repeated, approaching us, "I've got me some plump, ripe seeds at a good price, I do."

I eyed the seeds skeptically, thinking they looked anything but.

"Well no thanks to the seeds lass," I said, trying to keep the distaste for her handful of seeds out of my voice, "but thank you all the same. We've actually come looking for a-"

"Dammit!" she said, throwing the seeds to the ground.

Drostan and I looked at each other and then back to her. "I'm sorry," I stuttered around, "I meant no offense..."

"No," she answered after a moment or so, having calmed down, "it's fine. I wouldn't want them either," she said, wiping her eyes, which had begun to moisten with tears. "It's a lie, sure enough: *plump, ripe seeds*. They're worthless, dried up seeds!" Then she added in a disheartened tone, "That's all we can find round here."

Apparently, our confusion was visible enough for her to continue with a little more clarity. "I used to work for Seed Incorporated. Pretty much *everybody* in Exploit works there, except for those of us what works the streets. Now I spend all hours looking for seeds and people what needs them. Stolen seeds, discarded seeds, lost seeds; whatever I get me mitts on." Then, pointing up to a billboard, she added, "They say they'll change your life."

Drostan and I looked up and read the familiar pitch:

> *With three simple tools, Seed Inc. can change your life. All that's required is a little faith in the product we provide; hope for a providential future by means of our product; and our product itself: The Seed.*

"Changed my life alright," she said, now standing directly in front of us. "I hate these bloody seeds, but it's all I got now."

We were silent for a moment.

"It's going to be alright, lass," Drostan finally said, in a shaky attempt at consolation.

She defiantly snapped her eyes to his, "What do *you* know?"

"I just mean, things can, work out, somehow..."

I honored his attempts, but my brother's heart was much bigger than his brain at the moment, so I threw him a line. "What my brother means to say is that we both offer you our services if there's anything we can do to help."

Her defiance seemed to soften as she looked back and forth to both of us. "D'you mean that?"

We glanced to each other and back with simultaneous nods, "Aye."

She gave a long, awkward pause, looking at the ground and

back up again, before sort of embarrassedly, quietly saying, "I'm sorry I tried to bait you."

"Think nothing of it, lass," I said with a smile. "We won't."

"Now," chimed in Drostan, "will you let us buy you lunch?"

"Wow," she said with a smile. "You two are right *gentlemen*, aint'ya guv?"

"Well, *he* might be," I grinned, looking at my brother. "I've only got about two pounds fifty."

"You bought the pastries; I'll buy lunch," he said.

"Aye? Truly you *are* a gentleman."

"I like you two," laughed Crystal. And she led us to the nearest café.

Chapter Four

"So, you're telling me that there's a place what's built from hand-crafted stone, and plum covered with beautiful, green plants?"

"Aye," I answered, sipping my coffee.

We sat talking in a little side street burger bar. I didn't quite like the look of the place; dirt and grease covered every available surface and the proprietor looked very questionable, like the kind of guy who would spit in your food to add flavoring. But Crystal had assured us that it was one of the cleanest places in Exploit, so we did our best to ignore our disgusting surroundings and have a good meal. Or at least, *a* meal, as it were.

"Well, hey," she said with half a laugh, pointing to her clean plate, "thanks for the burger and chips, but you didn't have to buy me lunch to tell me fairy tales. Actually," she redirected, "I suppose it was a good idea to buy me lunch, cause I probably would'a left you standing in the street with a load of bollocks like that, *magic vines* not withstanding. No offense."

"None taken, love," I replied, "but it's not bollocks. It's true every word."

"We can take you there if you like," added Drostan. "Well,

assuming we can find the jewel first."

"Jewel?" this seemed to grab her immediate attention.

"See," began Drostan, "the Shepherd; the first shepherd, the Shepherd of the Gate; he asked us to find a precious jewel. He lost it, I guess."

"Why do you care?" she interrupted. "*You* didn't lose it."

"The Kingdom is a beautiful place," I added. "And the Shepherd was kind enough to let us through the gate to enter it, so we're happy to do him such a small favor. Plus," I added reflectively, "there's just something about him that makes you want to, you know, do things for him."

"Makes sense, I suppose," she said thoughtfully.

"You see, Crystal, here's the thing," continued Drostan, "Apparently, nothing in the Kingdom is lost, so we had to go somewhere else to find the lost jewel."

"That's why we're here in Exploit," I added.

"We need to-"

"I know where a *stolen* jewel is," she interrupted.

We both stared at her.

"What's that?" I finally asked.

"A diamond. About as big as me fist. It's Mr. Jobs'." She said his name with the sort of reverence that comes from fear. She swallowed then looked at us. Apparently, he was also someone she expected us to know, which we, of course, did not.

"Mr. Jobs?" Drostan asked, prompting her to continue.

She swallowed again. "It's a long story," she said, nervously picking at a scab on one of her knuckles.

"We've got time," I consented.

For a minute, we weren't sure if she was going to talk, then she finally gave a big sigh and looked up.

"When I worked for Seed Incorporated, just barely getting by I was. It's not the rich, lavish lifestyle they makes it out to be, you know. My employment was um, terminated because I was stealing seeds; some for meself, some to push on the street." She looked up to see how we were taking her story. Then she continued.

"So I was forced to work the street for keeps, and things got pretty bad. Like I said before, seeds is scarce out here, and the ones what you find is old and dried up. It's right hard to make a living that way, sure *enough*.

"So anyway, once out on the street, I didn't know what to do with meself. I was starving, you see; can't live without food, yeah? So I goes into this restaurant, Eddie's Diner I think it was, but I goes in the back like. I walks in and grabs a loaf of bread is all, but the owner grabs me before I can get away, says I got to sit and wait for Mr. *Jobs*." She shuddered as she said his name.

"Come to find out, Mr. Jobs is like some *boss*-man of all the muscle in this town, which he partners to certain restaurants and businesses. He provides protection, or whatever it is he provides, and skims off the top profits of said establishments; got me, guv?"

We nodded.

She shifted in her seat as if she were finally getting into her story, "So I'm sitting here, in this kitchen like, waiting for some boss-man; who knows what he'll do to me; so I gets a bit jumpy, yeah? But right when I'm about to make my getaway like, I sees him come in, all three-piece-suit and the like, with goons on each side.

"What's this I hear about trouble?" he says.

"Stealing bread," says the owner, pointing to me, and Jobs walks over, all big and scary like.

"I'll give you two choices," says Jobs, "I can put you back in the street naked and bloody, or you can pay for the bread and come work for me."

"Work for you?" I says.

"Yeah," he says. "You can be one of my girls. I can always use another."

And so I says, "What's *one of your girls*?"

And he says, "You'll know when I tell you. What's it gonna be, babe?"

Now understand, I'm not a huge fan of being called babe, but I'm not a huge fan of being *naked and bloody* either, so I goes with Jobs to his car and he takes me back to his mansion like. So I'm all looking around at this huge place and I'm like, "You live here?!"

"So do you now," says Jobs. And he takes me down to *The Warehouse*, like a dungeon underneath the mansion, and he points out a pole, in the back like. "People who owe me money spend their nights down here, tied to this pole," he says. "But people I like," and he touches my nose, "like you, babe; people I like sleep in nice, big, soft beds with satin sheets upstairs."

So, long story not much shorter, I went from rags to bloody riches for snagging a loaf of bread.

It didn't take me too long to figure out that being *one of Jobs' girls* meant that I could have anything I wanted; so long as I did certain favors for Mr. Jobs. Like if he wanted me out on the street for a day selling seeds, I'd get dolled up and spend the day doing that. Or some days I'd have to spend out, on the arm of him or one of his rich partners, for club appearances and whatnot.

And, being one of the girls, I'd spend at least one day a week *in*; his *private companion* and all that. Mind you, that wasn't my favorite, but I didn't mind it too much, at least not at first. Remember, I came from nothing; having everything was kinda nice, even when I had do favors I didn't like.

Some days in, I don't know why, but Mr. Jobs would be in an extra-good mood; he'd treat me like a *lady*, like I was *important*. It didn't happen very often, for sure, but one time, when he was in one of those moods, he took me into the back of his office. Normally, this was off limits; reserved for meetings of a private nature, with partners and investors and the lot.

He opened a little door what looked like a closet, and I saw that it was secret stairs. He took me down the secret stairs to a place in The Warehouse that I'd never seen: a vault. That's when he showed me the diamond. I never seen nothing like that before. It was brilliant.

"If anyone ever tried to take this," says Jobs, "I'd put them on the pole, or worse. You know why?"

"Why?" says I.

"Because it's mine," says Jobs. "It's beautiful and it's mine. It's important to me, so I protect it. Just like you, babe. I protect you because you're beautiful and you're mine."

It was sweet, I thought, but as time got by, I figured out that my being *his* wasn't exactly all it was cracked up to be. I got tired of being his girl, having to do his favors; having nice clothes and all this, but still feeling like trash. So I says to meself, if I'm going to *feel* like a street girl, I might as well be a *free* one, yeah?

So I up and left one night; left the nice meals, the satin sheets, nights at the clubs, where the men take your coat and pull out your chair; I left it all for the street. And now here I am, just like you're seeing me: eating a free meal on a stranger's quid cause I'm skin-and-bones-starving-away, trying to make ends meet selling dried up, worthless seeds."

Drostan and I just sort of sat there for a moment, looking at Crystal.

"You've been through a lot, lass," I said.

She looked uncomfortable with the compassion in my words, as if it were something that should not be reserved for *her*. "Yeah, I suppose. But I'm making it though."

"Crystal," began Drostan apprehensively, "are you afraid to go back there?"

Her look briefly said yes, but she shrugged it off and said,

"Hadn't really thought about it. I got no reason to go back."

"But if you *had* a reason, I mean. Would it be dangerous?"

"Oh, I don't know, I guess it could be maybe; probably not though. But like I says, I got no reason."

"...If the diamond is *stolen* anyway," I thought aloud, "then taking it to the Shepherd wouldn't really be stealing, it would be more like returning stolen property, no?"

"Aye," Drostan mumbled in agreement, having shared the thought.

"Whoa, wait up," interrupted Crystal, the fear coming out more clearly now. "You're not actually considering going in and taking it, are you?"

"We came here to find a lost jewel. If this is it, then we need to try and get it." I paused to try and read her expression. "Will you take us there?"

She jumped out of her seat. "Are you out of your bloody brain?! Were you not paying attention this whole time?! Jobs is- Going back at all is one thing, but making a quick smash n'grab to steal the one thing he cares about most, that's bloody suicide!"

"Aren't you sick of your life here?" Once Drostan realized he'd said it, it was too late to stop the words.

Crystal looked down to the table for a moment and then back up again, tears welling up in her eyes. "You *know* that I am..."

"I don't mean to be insensitive, lass," he said after a moment's silence, reaching across the table to touch her arm. "I'm only saying, we can take you back with us to the Kingdom, help you start a new life." He let that sit for a moment before he continued, "But we can't leave this place without the lost jewel. If you help us, we'll be free to help you."

After a long awkward silence, Crystal sat back down. Quietly looking down, she finally said, "Okay," with a little smile that mixed courage and fear, "I'll do it."

We quickly finished then left the café and made our way through the city of Exploit, following Crystal down dirty alleyways and narrow sidewalks. It was a dismal city. Big, wide cracks ran all the way up the sides of the buildings, separating large, discolored patches of wood or stone. The dim sun shone through the smog of the sky, silhouetting the buildings whose shadows surrounded us.

"Jobs usually goes to the restaurants for meetings in the mornings, so we'll probably get in and out without too much a problem." Her whispered tone somehow seemed to negate her confident words.

"What about his men?" Drostan asked.

"His goons aren't the *smartest*, you know." These words were spoken without the trace of fear she had when speaking of Jobs. "I'll get us in."

Once the day had progressed to evening, as we had spent it moving across the city, she assured us that it was too late to do anything that day, so we rented a room for the night, giving Crystal the bed while Drostan and I took the floor. When the sun rose, we made our way somberly once again through the alleyway maze of Exploit.

When we finally did arrive at the mansion, we had to stop in awe. *Mansion* was definitely an appropriate word. It might as well have been Lennoxlove, the kind of place foreigners tour when they're on holiday.

Same as Crystal had been when she first saw it; I was amazed at the grandeur of this place. The grounds alone were more lavish than anything I'd ever seen, much less the house itself. The artistic lawn perfectly set up the stately, three-storied home. It was overwhelming. And though it was a very handsome establishment, everything about its walls and doors said, "not welcome."

Crystal snuck us up through the long, Greco-decorated front lawn, weaving from statue to statue. We had to duck under bushes, hide behind fountains; it was actually quite exciting.

We made our way up to the veranda and around to the side porch, climbed over the hand-carved wooden railing, and quietly climbed through the small window into the drawing room. It was lined with huge bookshelves, stretching to the ornately-painted ceiling, stacked full with books which appeared as though they were more for décor than for reading.

Down through the long, back hall we stepped silently, from the drawing room to the kitchen, gladly neither hearing nor seeing anyone. Each doorway we passed opened up to an empty room, still and calm with only furniture as its company, until the last door, which was barely cracked open. As we passed it, I saw through the crack that it closed off a dark, downward staircase, and I knew that it must have been the door to The Warehouse.

Mounted to the wall on the opposite side of the door, where the hallway wall met the kitchen, there was a plaque. I stopped for a moment to notice it. Engraved deep into its thick, beautiful, gold plate were these words: *May the Foundation of My Castle Be the Bones of My Debtors.*

These words, obviously intended to ignite fear, stirred in me a different emotion.

Thinking on the sadness stirred in me by this man's seemingly unquenchable love of money, I continued with Crystal and my brother through the back of the kitchen, into the adjacent hall, and up the stairs to the second floor.

Finally arriving at the big, formidable office door, we looked at each other and then back to it as if it were sealing off a dreaded monster. Crystal cracked it open and the three of us entered the room to find a huge man sitting behind the even bigger desk. Looking up from the money he was counting, he looked to be almost as surprised to see us as we were to see him.

"Babe," he said, after a long awkward pause, pressing a little red button on his desk, "it's good to have you back." Then I knew we were facing Jobs himself.

She looked scared for a moment, but glancing back at us, seemed to gain courage from our presence. "Crystal," she said. "It's *Crystal.* And I'm *not* back."

He looked chagrinned for a moment, but quickly regained his arrogant confidence when two big men stepped in from the hallway and stood behind us.

"You need something, Boss?" one of them asked.

"Escort these gentlemen out to the street, however you should choose is fine, and introduce our lady friend to the pole." Then he turned to look at Crystal, "I figured you would've learned before; what's mine is always mine."

That's when I felt a crack on the back of my head.

Chapter Five

I woke up in the street next to my brother who was still unconscious. I had no idea how long I'd been out, but I figured it had been awhile.

"Wake up, Dros," I said, rustling my brother to consciousness.

"Bloody hell, my head," he sat up, rubbing the back of his head. "Suppose we were caught."

"Looks like," I agreed.

"Where's Crystal?"

"Last I can remember, Mr. Jobs said something about the pole..."

"The pole!" said Drostan with alarming realization. "She's probably tied up right now! We have to save her!"

"Aye."

"But we don't know how to get to her..." he said, still in a panic.

"I *do* actually," I said reflectively. "I saw the door to The Warehouse in the hallway."

"Yeah dancer!" he said, tightening his fist in victory. And then his face sobered again, "But how do we get back in without being found again?"

"I suppose that'll take some careful planning... Have you got any ideas?"

He thought for a moment. "A distraction..."

"Aye?"

"-Out in the lawn like, to get the guards' attention."

"So we can sneak into the mansion."

"Aye."

"Aye, that's good. What though? It would need to be something big enough to get the attention of at least most of them."

"How many?"

"Earlier it looked like there were about, I don't know, fifteen, twenty maybe..."

Drostan thought hard for a moment, while I watched the little gears turn in his head. Finally, I saw the light bulb click on.

"I've got it," he said, bright-eyed. "Remember the summer before Ma died; our prank in the McMillan barn?"

"Aye," I laughed, remembering younger years. "That's a good idea."

"Except no fire this time," we agreed simultaneously.

"Aye, but what about the garden hose?" Drostan added.

"We can use the fountain in front of the mansion."

"How?"

"I'll show you..."

And so we got up off the ground and began treading the city for the biggest wooden box we could find.

Eventually we found a grocery with a nice owner who was

willing to give us a used, ten-gallon tomato box. We lined the inside of it with the card-stock produce dividers he'd also given us, to make it more solid like, and headed back toward the mansion to save Crystal.

Once back at the head of the long lawn, I crawled as quickly and quietly as I could to about the middle, where the fountain was, and Drostan followed with the box. After peeking up over the fountain's big, deep base to ensure that no guards were looking in our direction, at least, not *exactly* our direction, I stood up on the brim to look into the water spout at the top to make out its approximate shape. Following my assessment, I scoured the ground for just the right rock, as my brother watched, wondering what I was doing.

After a few moments, I found a jagged rock about the size of a golf ball that formed a rudimentary point at one end. I hoisted myself back up and jammed the rock into the spout, causing the water to spray up in a strait, steady stream.

"Aye," said Drostan quietly to himself with a smile, "brilliant."

"The fountain being this far away from the mansion," I whispered, "I'm hoping they won't notice until it's time..."

I checked around again, to each of the guard posts up at the mansion, to ensure that this had not caught their attention. To my delight, none had seemed to notice.

"You're up," I whispered, handing him Donald Baggs' matchbook and blackjacks from my pocket.

Drostan set the lined, wooden box on its side to the left of the fountain, aiming the open end toward the mansion to guarantee that the loud echo that would be created inside the box was directed toward our target audience. Then, plugging my ears, I watched as Drostan lit the inter-twisted wicks of the wad of blackjacks and then plugged his ears.

The popping sound was almost deafening, even with my thumbs in my ears. After the several quick blasts, Drostan grabbed the box to hide behind a statue and we quickly snuck back the way we'd come, from statue to statue. Now that most of the guards had been adequately distracted, believing they'd heard some sort of electrical explosion, or whatever it was that had "broken the Boss's fountain," we were able to go the long way around and sneak in as we'd done earlier with Crystal.

With most or all of the guards occupied in the front lawn, we crept quietly down the hallway, and checked thoroughly the stairwell to The Warehouse before descending. No guards were anywhere near as far as we could tell, and we saw Crystal tied to the pole just as we'd suspected she would be.

"You made it!" she yelped happily.

"Shh!" warned Drostan. "We don't know who might be close enough to hear."

"Oh, right," she said, hushing her voice. "Mum's the word, bruv."

We untied her as quickly as we could, and once her hands were free, she grabbed Drostan by the back of the neck and kissed him. "Thanks for coming to rescue me."

Drostan turned a bit red. "My pl- our pleasure," he answered, with an awkward little crack in his voice.

"We better be going," I said, looking at Drostan with the kind of knowledgeable smile that twin brothers hate.

"Aye," he agreed, not daring to look at me.

We took Crystal up the stairs to the ground floor, and upon reaching the top of the stairs, we turned to go back through the hall. We stopped dead in our tracks, seeing three big, armed guards staring back at us from the end of the hall. I made my decision quickly to take the lead, grabbing the other two each by the arm and darting off in the opposite direction, through the kitchen. I could hear the guards following us as we toppled pots, pans, and stools to slow them down.

Exiting the opposite end of the kitchen, we burst through the doors and entered the long dining room. Before we had even realized it, we sprinted past the end of the table, whose back faced the door we'd just exited, and whose chairs seated none other than Jobs and four more of his guards. Still running toward the opposite end of the dining room, I turned my head back to see the five of them jumping up, leaving their meals to chase us. Just as this happened, the previous three guards entered the room from the kitchen, joining the chase.

I barreled through the dining room door into the Gallery, looking for any sort of escape route. Had I the time to take it all in, I would have enjoyed perusing the entire room. Artworks from several centuries, from paintings to sculpture, were on elaborate display. It was the perfect demonstration of arrogant luxury. Jobs seemed to care only for power and money, and yet he had a two-story room dedicated to antiquity that few others than he could afford. And with little more than a moment to think about it, I ran for the second floor, by means of the spiral stair in the far corner.

Our feet clanged up the thin, metal stairs as we spun around the center pole from bottom to top, at least a good twenty feet ahead of our pursuers. Reaching the top, I was relieved to find that there were no guards on the second floor of the Gallery.

In my oblivious hurry, I didn't even glance at the artwork in the 2nd floor of the Gallery as I ran through it. Looking ahead of me, I saw that almost straight across from the top of the spiral stair was another door. I motioned for Drostan and Crystal to follow me and barged through the door.

The three of us stopped instantly, finding ourselves standing in some sort of dimly lit pool hall. A full room of gambling, drinking, cigar smoking gangsters seemed to stop everything and turn to look at us. There were pool games, card games, marbles, dice; anything that could be gambled upon was in play, and we had interrupted them all.

Easily enough, everyone seemed to go right back to what ever hand or scam he may have been working, and the noise and bustle of the room went right back to what it was just before we'd entered.

"There's a relief," said Drostan.

"Aye," I answered, "now let's not make an event of this. We'll just casually make our way to that door," I nodded to a door at the far left of the room.

We sort of worked our way in that direction, smiling and nodding, checking out this game or the next, trying not to appear that we were here by accident. As we moved through the room, we noticed, adding to the unsettling thoughts presented by a room full of gangsters, that just about every single one of them had a gun sitting on the table next to him.

About halfway to our destination, Jobs and his men finally crashed the party. This time, as it was obvious they had arrived on serious business, the bustle of the room came to an unmistakable halt.

Around the room, I heard a "Jobs" here, or an "Evening Jobs" there. These greetings, or rather recognitions of the host's entrance, continued around the room, as Jobs returned "hello" nods to several different men, being as cordial a host as possible given the circumstances, all the while scanning the room for us.

As this host-to-guest transaction was taking place, we were doing our best to stay hidden by a group of men standing at one of the pool tables. I knew it could only last for a moment, and he eventually saw us.

"Somebody grab those three!" yelled Jobs. That's when the unprecedented happened.

Like clockwork, without even thinking, as if it were something we'd rehearsed, my brother and I each grabbed a gun from one of the tables and stood back to back with Crystal between us.

"The lights!" I shouted, and my brother and I began shooting out each of the lights.

Strangely, like a flashback, this reminded me of more frivolous times. Two young lads shooting a pellet gun at Old Man Campbell's apples, set on a fencepost, or even still hanging from a tree. We'd best each other, pacing farther away with each turn. We'd each gained quite an eye, Da had said.

Then, we were lads learning to be men, but now, standing back to back in this pool hall with Crystal between us, we were crazy men with guns, or at least, that was the impression we were trying to project. And apparently it worked; we seemed to gradually clear a path to the door, and by the time the room was pitch-black, we were out in the hallway.

Just across the hall, facing the door we'd closed behind us was a window overlooking the back porch. The roof of the dining room below provided just enough overhang that we could stand on it outside the window, so we climbed out.

Standing on the ledge, I thought aloud, "We've got nowhere to go but up."

"So let's go up a bit quicker, yeah?!" said Crystal in a panic.

I hoisted myself to the second roof and then pulled Drostan up, who pulled Crystal up after. No sooner did we make it up than Jobs and his men were coming out the window as well.

"What now?" asked Crystal, trembling, as one at a time, Jobs and his men climbed onto the roof, backing us toward the very ledge.

And then suddenly, like a light-bulb flashing on in my brain, I remembered and acted before I could truly stop to think about it.

"Hawk!" I called as loudly as I possibly could, and heard my echo reverberating across the lawn. Following the last echo, I heard nothing but the pounding of my pulse in my ears.

Drostan, though still very concerned with Crystal's safety, mocked my efforts, doing his best to make light of the situation, "It seems these days you can't even depend on a huge talking bird."

Just then, I heard a deafening shriek, along with the flapping of enormous wings. In a quick jolt, the three of us turned our heads in the direction of the shriek. My heart was revived as I saw our rescue.

As Hawk swooped toward us, I saw his large talons stretching out, preparing to grab us. Seconds before he made contact, he yelled to my brother, "Pick her up!"

Drostan swept Crystal off her feet, cradling her tight in his arms.

"Oh no..." said Crystal, fearing what she could tell was about to happen.

And then, quickly and yet very delicately, as if careful not to scratch my back or neck, Hawk bunched up the back of my shirt into his talons, and I was lifted from the rooftop. I looked to my right to see my brother in the same position in Hawk's other foot, holding Crystal in his arms, who hung onto him for dear life, hiding her face in his chest.

Hawk soared high above the city and seemed to climb even

higher as he soared. It wasn't long before we'd entered the clouds, and my brother and I glanced to each other with the same question, and so I asked it.

"Hawk," I called up.

"Yeah?"

"Where are we going?"

"The land of true freedom."

"The States?" asked Drostan with half a smile. Even at a time like this, he couldn't help himself.

"Where?" I asked again after a moment, ignoring my brother.

"The vine to the Kingdom."

"But the Kingdom's *that* way," I said, pointing down toward the vine by the factory.

"There are no real directions out here, son."

"…Oh." It didn't make sense, yet his tone and confidence left me with a feeling of *right*.

Suddenly, I heard a shriek, louder and far more violent than Hawk, coming from behind us. I tried to see what it was, but before I could crane my neck around, it flew beneath us.

A strange sense of fear shot through me as I looked down at its back. Whatever it was had dark red, scaly skin; long, dark, boney wings; and a long, sharp-looking tail. As I glanced at his pointed, scaly head, we made eye contact. In his intense, obsidian eyes, I saw a more hatred than I'd ever seen.

Then I saw his nostrils flare, and a huge ball of fire shot up from his mouth with a shriek, barely missing us.

"What's happening?!" yelled Drostan.

"That's the Dragon!" answered Hawk, thrusting his wings through the air all the harder. "He doesn't want you to leave!"

"Why not?!"

"He doesn't want *anyone* to leave Exploit! Hang on!"

Hawk swooped as far up and away as he could from the Dragon into the clouds, and released us from his talons. This caused Drostan to let go of Crystal, who began screaming at realizing that she was free-falling through the sky.

I stretched my hands out in front of me as one normally does when falling, but instead of falling through the clouds as I expected, I landed atop a cloud on my hands and knees. After seeing that Crystal and my brother had also landed safely, the three of us peered over the edge of the cloud to see Hawk flying full speed back toward the Dragon.

The Dragon again hurled flames at Hawk, which Hawk dodged with little effort, swooping to one side, around, and underneath the giant, scaly beast. The Dragon, being too long, couldn't redirect his body in time to face Hawk, and so Hawk was able to swoop in and slice all eight talons into his enemy's underbelly.

The Dragon winced, whipping his tail around to catch Hawk in the face, launching him several feet away. Having our protector out of his way, the giant reptile turned his attention back to the three of us and with two hard thrusts of his bony wings, zoomed toward us.

"What now?!" Drostan yelled to me in a panic, standing nobly in front of Crystal to block her from any possible flames.

Hawk needs a diversion, I thought. "Just look after her!" I yelled to Drostan, and then dove off the cloud into the open air.

"Branan!" I heard them scream.

Immediately regretting my decision, I yelled in the most heightened sense of emergency that I could gather, "Hawk!" But I didn't see him anywhere.

I sped through the air for mere seconds before crashing into the Dragon. As I felt my ribs crack against his face, I reached my arms around his muzzle. Clenching tight my wrist with the opposite hand, I slid down to the beast's neck, where I held tight position.

The Dragon shrieked angrily, spewing flames in every direction, while somersaulting backward through the air. Though I was very afraid, I was happy to have distracted the beast from my brother and Crystal. Furious that I was on his back, the Dragon chased his tail trying to get to me.

Apparently, this was exactly the diversion Hawk needed. In my peripheral, I saw him sailing in on the Dragon's flank. When his talons connected, sinking into the red scales, the impact was so heavy that I was thrown from the beast up into the air. The Dragon winced with a blood-curdling shriek, blowing flames one last time before flying away in defeat.

Hawk caught me again by the shirt and carried me back to the cloud.

Drostan looked at me for a moment with somewhat of a misbelieving stare before finally saying, "Good bloody diversion..."

"I do what I can," I smiled. Then I turned to Hawk, "Thank

you, Sir."

"Aye," added Drostan and Crystal, "thank you."

Hawk nodded affirmatively. "We have just a way to go yet, whenever you're ready."

And so Crystal was again swept into Drostan's arms, and Hawk lifted us off our feet and carried us up and away.

Chapter Six

Standing on the cloud, I helped Crystal up from the vine, as my brother followed close behind. I watched Crystal's eyes as she stood atop the cloud and looked out over the gorgeous meadow.

"Are those the fairies?" she asked, happily amazed.

"Aye," I smiled.

About that time, little Miss Charity fluttered up to us with somewhat a look of incredulity.

"You two again? And what's this? Oh good, you've brought another," she said, glancing to Crystal with only slightly hidden sarcasm.

As unwelcomed as she'd intended to imply that we were, the three of us couldn't help but smile to each other; she was such a *precious* wee thing.

"I don't know what you're all smiling about," she said, perturbed. "You're in for a wallop."

"What do you mean?" I asked, noticing how Crystal tried not to smile, her eyes never leaving the wee fairy.

"You're here to reenter the Kingdom, yes?"

"Aye."

"I never saw you leave in the first place," she frowned, her face gradually shifting from annoyance to alarm, "which means you didn't come through the meadow. You took a shortcut! Admit it!"

"Aye," I answered, a bit confused. "Not allowed, I take it?"

"Shortcuts are strictly forbidden. The Shepherd makes rules for the good of the sheep. If the sheep ignore the rules, they can be more easily deceived."

"Sheep?" I asked. "What are you talking ab-"

She ignored me and continued, "Shortcuts are given to *trick* the sheep, and the only reason to trick the sheep is to *trap* the sheep, and the only reason to trap the sheep is to *eat* the sheep-"

"What are you talking about?!" the three of us interrupted simultaneously.

"The Wolf."

"The Wolf?" I asked smiling. "I thought he ate the pigs, not the sheep."

She glared at me in her tiny anger, "Sometimes he wears sheep's clothing; sometimes he even dresses as the Shepherd, but he is still a wolf."

These things came together in my head. "So the other shepherd- the one who showed us to the vine-"

"Yes. He tricked you into thinking he was helping you. That's what he does."

"But nothing bad happened," interjected Drostan. "As a matter of fact, *good* came of it; we were able to rescue Crystal." At this, I noticed Crystal's hand slide into Drostan's as he spoke, and it pleased me to see that they were quite taken with one another.

"Siding with the Wolf doesn't *always* end in harm," Charity interjected, not seeing nor caring about the beautiful connection I'd seen between my brother and Crystal, "and at times like these, he gains trust, which is worse than harm."

"We haven't *sided* with the-"

"Just," she interrupted, her face shifting back from alarm to annoyance, "stay away from the Wolf. Now, follow me so that I may introduce *her* to the Shepherd," and she turned and fluttered on, leading us up and over the soft, grassy hills toward the gate.

"Hello, little Miss Holiday," greeted the smiling Shepherd, once we'd arrived at the gate.

"Charity, my lord," she said, just as before, trying somewhat to conceal her irritation. My brother and I passed a silent, snickering glance to one another.

"Ah yes," answered the Shepherd, with a knowing glance to Drostan and I, "Charity. What may I do for you, my beautiful, little friend?"

"Thank you, my lord," she exchanged the pleasantry only out of custom. "However unaccustomed as it may be, I ask that I may have leave of this particular duty to pursue others which need my attention, as these two gentlemen, with whom you are previously acquainted, may do it justice."

The Shepherd seemed to be almost even holding back a laugh at the fairy's smugness, which seemed to irritate her all the more, and so he nodded and waved her on, sending her mumbling and fluttering off into the distance.

After she was gone from safe hearing distance, the Shepherd let out the breath he'd been holding with a quick little laugh. "I shouldn't do that," he said, "I know; they *hate* it when I misname them, but I can't help that it makes me chuckle every time."

The three of us shared an uneven, slightly awkward chuckle with him, at seeing an ornery streak through an individual whom we'd held to such a high level of prestige.

"And who is this?" he asked, finally noticing Crystal as a new face.

"Uh, this is, she's from," stuttered Drostan, "this is Crystal, Mister, um, Mister, Shepherd, Sir."

"Just Shepherd, son," he laughed. "You can call me Shepherd."

"Right…"

"Let us have a look at you, lass." Then, for the first time, Crystal looked into the Shepherd's eyes.

Something changed. I didn't know what it was; perhaps only Crystal and the Shepherd knew, but something felt different. Drostan glanced at me in a way that showed he could feel it as well.

"You've lost yourself, haven't you, lass?" said the Shepherd in a tender, quiet voice, his eyes, still locked on Crystal's. "You've no idea who you are anymore. Am I right?"

There was a long, quiet pause, and I saw two big tears stream down her face, before she answered in a soft, cracked voice, "…Yes."

He waited for a moment, out of sensitivity, and then continued, "Do you know how it happened?"

"…I tried to use my seeds to *earn* happiness."

"But, deep down, you knew that could never work..."

Crystal was quiet for a moment, before her shoulders began to tremor as, though still silently, she cried harder.

"Yes," she said, burying her face in her hands, "I knew."

At this, the Shepherd wrapped his arms around her and held her as she cried. Sad as it was, still it was beautiful; as though they were father and daughter, long departed and now reunited. Drostan and I of course, standing there, feeling awkwardly intrusive, had nothing to do but wait, or so I supposed anyway.

After several minutes, Crystal's quiet crying stilled to peace, and the Shepherd pulled her out of his arms.

"And now," he said, smiling, "I have a seed for you that shall be your *own*." And he placed a very green, very healthy seed in her palm. Looking to my brother and me, he added with a knowing brow, "I trust your seeds have produced for you a good harvest?"

"Uh..." we both stammered. "We still have them," I added, as we each pulled a seed from the pockets of our jeans.

"This I know," he answered with a flat smile.

"-We've actually been occupied since we first arrived," offered Drostan, "looking for your jewel as we promised."

"Aye," answered the Shepherd with a disappointed look not so hidden in his smile, "*busyness* has been the waste of many a seed..."

Drostan and I awkwardly glanced to one another, feeling somewhat ashamed, though we didn't totally understand why.

"We found it," added Drostan, trying to lighten the mood. "The jewel, that is."

But then I added in a lower, more disappointed tone, "But we weren't able to bring it back."

"The jewel you speak of is not the one I sent you to find," said the Shepherd, with his bright smile returning. "But I thank you all the same for trying to do what you thought was right by me."

"The diamond wasn't yours?"

"Nor do I desire it," he smiled, concealing a snicker.

"Then I'm glad we didn't work extra hard to try to steal it," added Drostan dryly, to which the Shepherd laughed more hardily at our expense than I thought truly necessary.

"But as you two young men can see," continued the Shepherd, lifting Crystal's hands in his own, "your journey was not a loss, for this lovely Crystal has been given a new beginning." He looked at us solemnly, "For that, I thank you both. You have done well."

"You're welcome," we both said awkwardly, each wondering why *he* should thank *us*.

"And now," he added, "let me show you my garden." And before we could ask any questions, he turned and started walking. We expected him to walk through the large gate, but to our surprise, he continued past it. Of course, we didn't know what else to do, so we followed him.

"We're not going in?" I asked.

"Sadly," he answered, "the quickest route to my garden is often times to go out and around the Kingdom altogether." We shrugged and followed behind him.

We walked the outer wall all the way around the Kingdom, and

I was surprised at realizing how big it was. When inside the Kingdom, the wall that surrounded it wasn't really visible. Well, I'm sure I probably could have seen it had I looked for it, but I guess it was just easier to take for granted that it was there.

"So this stone wall surrounds the *entire* Kingdom?"

"Yes, son," the Shepherd answered me. "Had I not fortified my Kingdom, my sheep would not be safe."

"But," began Drostan respectfully, "what about the Wolf? How'd he get in?"

"I suppose he came in the back gate."

"There's a back gate?"

"Indeed."

Drostan stared blankly at the Shepherd, "But… With all due respect, Sir, what good is the wall then?"

"The Wolf has no power to enter unless he is invited."

"But who would do that?" asked Crystal.

"Any sheep whom the Wolf has deceived."

As we continued walking, I thought about that. Drostan and I had been deceived, and rather easily at that. I thought about that as well. Why had Drostan and I been deceived? We were usually quite perceptive.

I remembered how much I'd been dreading retracing our many steps back through the Kingdom. The Wolf's suggestion to take his vine had seemed so easy that we were both quick to choose that way. I wondered how often the Wolf was able to infiltrate the Kingdom because of someone's wanting a shortcut to something they wanted.

"Where is your garden?" asked Crystal, interrupting my reverie.

"There," said the Shepherd, pointing off to the foggy distance. "Spring Mountain."

My heart fell, thinking about walking all that way.

"Wow," breathed Drostan. "We're going way up there?"

"Aye, but don't worry; nothing will harm you when you're with me."

"Why, is it dangerous?" I asked. *Great,* I added internally, and I thought the *walking* was the bad part.

"There are many obstacles to keep the sheep from my garden, or more would come."

"Um," Drostan began with an awkward pause, "I mean no disrespect, sir, but why should we trudge all this way and risk danger just to see a garden?"

The Shepherd came to a stop, and smiled as he explained, "I do not mandate that you follow me, but *I am* going to my garden. I welcome you to come, in faith that your visit will be worth your journey, but again, I will not demand it of you. You may certainly find a place to be content if you stay here."

The three of us were quiet for a moment to consider what he'd said. It certainly seemed that he desired for us to come with him. And for all accounts, it seemed he had our best interest in mind. At that moment, with glances back and forth, we all three sort of non-verbally agreed to continue on with the Shepherd.

Then Drostan, returning to the previous topic, asked, "What kind of obstacles?"

"Diggers, Tree Sprites; you'd be surprised what kind of monsters work their way into the Kingdom."

"What are Diggers and Tree Sprites?" asked Crystal warily.

"Diggers live in the Drylands," the Shepherd motioned ahead, and I noticed that as we'd talked, we'd passed the stone wall's limits, crossed the Back Meadow, and were now only steps from entering a vast cracked terrain seemingly devoid of water.

The Shepherd continued, "The Diggers are strange, black-hearted creatures. Past happenings, past feelings, past hurts; these are their life-source. They will show you what they *will* you to see. You will hear what they *will* you to hear. They want inside your head."

"Wow," breathed Crystal. "And... er... the Tree Sprites?"

"Tree Sprites live in the Mountain Forests. They were once fairies of the Meadow, but they refused to do what they were commissioned. When I bade them choose: allegiance or exile, sadly, they chose exile. Though they hide from me in the Forests, they hate me in their hearts."

I noticed Drostan's expression change, as though this story had confused him.

"Again," he said, "I mean no disrespect-"

"You need never fear to speak with me plainly, son," the Shepherd interrupted.

"Well, Sir," Drostan continued, "you don't seem the type to

force someone to do something they don't want to do..."

"Indeed," the Shepherd paused thoughtfully before he continued. "And now I tell you something you may not understand: The fairies exist *solely* to be in my service, that the goings on of the Kingdom may continue as they have this past age."

"...Aye, right," Drostan agreed to the obviousness of the point, "but I don't understand."

"In time, son," the Shepherd chuckled to himself.

I considered all these things the Shepherd had told us, the four of us walking in silence as Drostan and Crystal, I assumed, were pondering the same. We continued walking in silence through the Drylands to the thick forest at the foot of Spring Mountain.

"The Tree Sprites won't come out?" asked Crystal in a worried tone.

"You needn't fear, lass," assured the Shepherd. "Just like the Diggers, the Sprites hide when I am near."

We continued up the mountain until the forest broke and we crested the steep incline. Atop the plateau, we saw a stone wall, similar to the wall around the Kingdom, but not as broad.

I looked down the wall in both directions, and as my eyes scanned the wall, I found no gateway of any kind.

"How do you get in?" thought Drostan aloud.

Without a word, the Shepherd stepped forward and turned to his right, opening a little door in the wall that would be hidden to anyone who didn't already know it was there. He welcomed us to follow as he ducked to step through the little doorway into a cramped, little stone alley.

After a couple little sharp turns, the tiny, stone alley opened up to a beautiful array of colors and shapes, beautiful plants growing in every direction. Mostly greens, the different shades of blue, red, purple, and yellow were just sort of peppered in here and there, and there seemed to be no pattern to the mess. And yet somehow, it was still breathtaking, overflowing with life, like the floor of a rainforest.

"This place," Drostan breathed, wide-eyed, apparently more inspired than I was, "makes me feel… more *alive* somehow."

"I've never seen anything so beautiful," whispered Crystal, and I turned to see that she was crying again.

"Thank you," said the Shepherd smiling, as strangely, one big tear rolled down his face. "I'm glad you like it."

Not really understanding the emotions I was witnessing, I tilted my head back to look up to the tops of the trees that surrounded the garden. Not so surprisingly in a magical place like this, the trees didn't seem to have tops at all. Rather, they all seemed to gradually merge together somewhere up a ways, forming a sort of opaque canopy, giving more the atmosphere of a *room* than a garden.

There was far too much for me to take it all in, much less explain, but several little things caught my eye.

I saw a bright yellow flower blooming from a base of black instead of green. Little bees buzzed about it, doing their busy little chores. The scene reminded me of the meadow fairies.

Hanging high from one of the trees, I saw a long vine, braided with three shades of green. Here and there, descending the vine, were tiny white sprouts, flowers barely budding.

The further I looked back into the trees, the further they seemed to go. And far back in the depths, seeming to fill in the dark empty spaces as it were, there was a mist that seemed to sort of hover. It looked as though it would smell sweet, the kind of morning mist that makes you feel fresh and clean. It reminded me of home.

These all were simple things; it was more the way in which these simple things were combined with innumerable other simple things that made the whole so beautiful.

As I said, my brother and Crystal seemed to be much more taken in by it all than I was. Understand, it was indeed an overwhelming sight, but I had other things on my mind at the time. Seeing all this life growing around me did little more than remind me of the seed in my pocket.

I didn't want to disappoint the Shepherd, having seen how great a man he was. I respected him, understand. I decided that I needed to come up with some type of plan, once I got back to the streets and markets of the Kingdom, to use my seed.

Chapter Seven

I stayed in the garden for a while, but I was eager to get back, to get to work on my plan for my seed and please the Shepherd. And so, once I left the Shepherd's garden, I walked the great stone avenue through the Kingdom in search of an open plot to purchase. My brother and Crystal had decided to stay awhile with the Shepherd in his garden, but I felt I could better honor his kindness by putting myself to work.

I eventually found a little empty lot just next to the shop of a very kindly gentleman nearly twice my age it would seem, a plow smith named Jack.

With Jack's friendly assistance, and the use of his wares, I opened the ground near the back corner of the small patch and planted the seed the Shepherd had given me.

As we worked together, I realized strait away that I liked this man Jack. Unlike most of the people of the Kingdom with whom I had thus far come into contact, he spoke very little.

He was not aloof by any means, understand; he simply chose not to fill the air with words of chatter. I supposed him a kind and sincere man, who would not presume to offer an opinion at every chance, but willing to give one in wisdom if asked.

Being pretty nearly completely uncertain as to what to do after my seed was to be firmly established in the ground, I broke the silence of our work with a thought on which I hoped he would venture an opinion.

"I suppose I should start setting up some sort of shop," I thought aloud, staring off toward the front of my lot.

"But do you know what seed you've been given?" asked Jack.

"No sir," I answered. "Why do you ask?"

"Well son, I think it unwise to begin an operation based on a plant you don't yet know..."

"...A valid point, sir... What do you suggest I do?"

He seemed a bit dumbfounded by my question, in that the answer was supposedly obvious, "I suppose you should wait."

"Wait?"

"For the seed to grow," he said with the same obvious expression. "Patience is by no means the favorite of options, but often times the only one."

And without thinking, I answered, "Thanks, but no. I leave patients to the infirmary."

"Aye," he chuckled.

"Oh," I caught myself, "I didn't suppose you'd catch that one. I assumed there'd be no need for the likes of an infirmary in the Kingdom."

"...Well I mean no disrespect to you son, but that's a silly assumption. Remember, the Kingdom is inhabited by the likes of *us*. You bleed when cut, don't you?"

"Once again, valid point."

"And besides," he continued, "Not all of us were *born* into this kingdom. Originally, I come from God's country, same as you."

"You're Scottish?"

"Aye. Perth."

"Dundee," I said, pointing to myself with a smile, "we're neighbors, fancy that."

"Indeed," he smiled, with an affirmative butt of the hand to my shoulder.

"...Something strange I've noticed..." I said after a moment.

"Aye?" his brow raised. "What's that?"

"Well, what is it that's different about..." I stammered, trying to find the words. "Well, you're more like my brother and I in a way that... Well, most of these Kingdom people are..."

I saw in Jack's eyes that he seemed to understand what I was trying to say, and he paused for a moment of silence to calculate an efficient response.

"If all you've ever known is one thing," he finally answered, "you may very well have the *purity* of that one thing, but you'll have very little ability to *relate* to anything from outside it."

My brow raised unconsciously at the gravity of the observation, "...Well spoken, Sir." I left the conversation where it lay, as well as my seed, and followed Jack to his shop.

"Have you any family?" I asked, as I helped him close the large, hinged shutter down over the counter window facing the street.

"Aye, a son and a daughter. We have a small home just over the ridge."

"Have you? And their mother?"

He paused for a moment, "Died last year."

I felt bad for asking. "I *do* apologize sir..."

He dismissed my apology with a wave of his hand, "Nah, you'd no way of knowing." He began scraping the soil off the plow blades, so I grabbed a knife and rag to help.

"What was her name, your wife?"

"Lashay." I saw his eyes defocus off into space as he quit scraping to reminisce in his inner world of memory. "A lovely woman she was... I remember when we first made the choice to join the Kingdom, wide eyed and ignorant," he said with a smile. "We thought it was a magical place of *perfection*, no pain, no loss. How foolish we were..."

"You regret your choice to come here?"

"Oh no, son," he answered, quickly focusing his eyes on mine. "Understand, I'd stand the same chance or more of loss *outside* the Kingdom, and that without the Shepherd's seeds." He pause with a shake of his head, "No, I could *never* regret the choice to come here."

"I'm sorry," I added, after a respectful pause, "but I still don't understand what the big deal is about seeds."

"Once again, *patience*," he said with a short laugh. "It's not something that can be explained. You'll understand in time."

After a short, awkward moment of silence, we both went back to scraping the blades.

"Your children?" I asked, trying to kill the awkwardness.

"I'm sorry?"

"Your son and daughter; what are their names?"

"Tommy and Cassia," he answered. "Twins; about your age, I should think."

"Twins?" I smiled. "My brother and I are twins."

"Identical?"

"Fraternal. We're very much alike though."

"Aye, as it usually goes. The same with mine."

"Be happy to meet them, should the opportunity arise."

Just then, I heard the creak of the little, wooden back door of Jack's shop. I turned and saw a beautiful woman step through and peer around the door. She had vibrant, red hair that hung down past her shoulders. To match her hair, her arms were sprinkled with freckles. Her eyes were a brilliant blue that seemed to bring in a new light to the room.

She smiled slightly to me as we made a moment's eye contact, before speaking to Jack, "Dinner's ready, Da."

"-Perhaps the opportunity has arisen," said Jack with a glance to me. "This is my daughter Cassia. Cassia, this is Branan."

"Pleased to meet you, Mr. Branan."

"Likewise," I answered, truly pleased.

"Will Mr. Branan be joining our table this evening, Da?"

"Aye, if it'd please him," his eyes sending the question to me.

"I accept and thank you," I said, passing a smile to each.

Cassia retreated back out the door to the house, and Jack noticed my notice of her.

"Has the spirit of her mother, that one," he said, returning my attention to him. "Amazing women both."

Jack and I finished scraping the blades before closing snug the back door of the shop behind us and retreating to the house.

The meal Cassia had prepared was delicious, and sitting around the table, the four of us conversed about whatever found its way into conversation; shoes and ships and ceiling wax, if I may quote the walrus.

I found Tommy to be a very agreeable man, much like my brother in many ways, it seemed. I noticed how he kept at all times a protective eye on his sister. Not that I believe he actually feared for her safety in any way, but simply as an unconscious measure of his love for her. In fact, the love between all three members of this family was almost tangible.

The four of us kept each other laughing whenever possible, very much enjoying the diversion. It was quite some while after we'd finished eating before the gravity of a serious topic fell on the table.

"The only thing to watch, son," Jack began, out of nowhere it seemed, "is not to waste time."

"What do you mean?" I asked.

"The Kingdom is a gracious place to sustain a living; the Shepherd of the Gate keeps a careful watch. But these accommodations cause many to float through time as if the diversions of living are the highest purpose."

I considered that for a moment. "So what is it?" I finally asked.

"Mmm?"

"The purpose? Beyond a living wage and a yearly goal of harvest, what *is* the purpose?"

"As per specifics, I can't tell you, lad. That's for each alone to understand. But overall, the ever-growing Kingdom is the purpose of itself."

There was a heavy silence, before Tommy broke it with a smile, "You'll have to forgive my da. He speaks in riddles, that one."

I laughed, but filed away in my mind what Jack had said, assured that it must have some deep importance.

Once it was obvious that little dialogue was yet to survive, Jack bade his son help him sharpen the three newest blades and made the suggestion, if I wouldn't mind, that I help Cassia with the dishes.

I eagerly obliged, though the gleam in his eye told me this was contrived; I wanted to speak with Jack's lovely daughter too much to mind some matchmaking. Not too incredibly awkwardly I'd hoped, I found myself moments later beside her at the sink.

I tried not to be awkward, but even more; I tried not to think on just how pretty she was. I barely knew this woman and my mind had no call to be racing through thoughts of settling down with her in a home here in the Kingdom; I put a stop to that as quickly as possible. The mind seems to often be a silly thing that, if you let it, will follow a thousand roads before you even notice it's left the house.

"So, you're new to the Kingdom?" she asked, handing me a

soapy dish to rinse.

"Aye, my brother and I arrived just, well, whenever it was. Time is hard to follow in this place..." my voice trailed off as I dried the dish.

"Do you like it here?"

"Sure. I mean, it's a nice place to visit."

"You won't stay?" She paused somewhat, I thought, significantly.

"For awhile perhaps, but I belong in Scotland... Don't you ever miss home?"

"This *is* home," she said, setting the dish she was scrubbing back into the soapy water and looking up at me. "I had a decent life in Perth, but *here* is where I belong. *Here* I have found purpose. Whether Highlands, Lowlands, or even *England*, God forbid," she smiled, "the place you call home shouldn't be merely where you're *from*, but where you *belong*. Are you sure you belong in the place you call home?"

"Well," I thought aloud, "It's where I was raised. I remember travels with Da to Inverness as a wee lad, hearing his pipes echo down through the glen, just like the song says... Those are my earliest memories. It's who I am."

"Aye," she said thoughtfully, returning the dish to its scrubbing, "maybe you're right. It's not my place to tell you your purpose."

A heavy, awkward silence filled the air, until I finally shattered it with the only thing I could think to say, "So what's yours?" I felt awkward as soon as I'd said it. That was a very heavy question for just getting to know someone.

"I'm sorry?"

Too late now, I'd already asked it. So I continued, "Your purpose; you said you've found purpose here. Is it okay to ask?"

"Oh, sure. I've found purpose and fulfillment in that I keep a home for my father, that he may spend his days working without a care of petty, household chores. And his work affords others the ability to harvest their seeds, thereby flourishing multiple harvests and expanding the Kingdom."

As she spoke, her beauty caught me off guard. I hadn't seen it fully until then, as she spoke so lightly and yet so selflessly of the one *small* way she was able to make a difference in the lives connected to hers, and I realized it *wasn't* so small after all.

She'd inspired me, and that was the tiny seed that began growing inside me to become more acquainted with this beautiful girl. I found myself leaning in a little closer as she continued.

"My father and brother would not have the time and energy to furnish such efficient plows as they do if I were not here to replenish them with hot meals and clean clothes. Often, *unseen* duties such as these afford the better recognized ones their ability to exist at all." She punctuated her speech by handing me another dish.

"Aye; a house stands on its foundation," I affirmed.

"...Well spoken," she smiled with a pleased look at my agreement, before taking another dirty dish from the counter.

Though the tone thus far had been slightly playful, I just couldn't keep the awe out of my voice. "Your servitude honors you," I said, watching her face as her eyes still awkwardly watched the dish she was washing. I tucked a tuft of stray red hair behind her ear, "You're all the more beautiful for it."

I could tell my boldness had caught her off guard, though she didn't look up from the soapy water, her face had turned as red as her hair. The silence that followed was only a few seconds, but its heaviness demanded I break it.

"I've been too forward," I said. "I apologize."

She said nothing, but scrubbed the dish a little more slowly, leaving more silence that I felt obligated to fill with my bumbling words.

"I only meant to pay you a compliment-"

"It's okay," she said, finally interrupting me with a shy little smile, before looking back down to the dishes. "Am I?" she added with a little blushing smile after a moment, still looking down into the water.

"Are you what?"

"Beautiful?"

"Aye." We exchanged glances, then she smiled and looked back down.

Just about that time, Jack and Tommy came back inside, for which I was grateful, as I had run out of words and not out of awkward silence.

"Thanks for helping out with the women's work, bother," said

Tommy with a friendly jab to my shoulder.

"Aye," I grinned, "maybe someday I'll be *man* enough to help with the plows."

"*'Maybe someday,'* he says," grinned Tommy to his father. "Sounds like this pup has a mind to be here awhile."

"I must admit, I've no *real* plans aside from setting up shop tomorrow," I smiled. "We'll see what happens from there, I suppose..."

"D'ya have a place to sleep, lad," asked Jack, slapping my back.

I didn't really know where Drostan and Crystal had been all day. I wondered where they would sleep tonight, but safely assumed they were still with the Shepherd. So when Jack offered me the couch to sleep for the night, I accepted with little worry for my previous company.

Once I had drifted to sleep, I dreamed of the little seed I had planted in the back of my lot. It was a very colorful, realistic dream.

I saw the little seed's taut flesh split open in two tiny points, and then three, then four, as the roots began sprouting. They grew down, pushing the soil apart as they searched for nourishment.

As this happened, similar sprouts began to grow from the top of the little seed. These stretched upward, eventually breaking the ground of a grassy pasture, seeking sunlight as they entered the open air.

Suddenly, a white bloom opened up with a flash of light, as the flower spread its petals out over the stem and soil. It continued to expand, growing down and gaining circumference across the surface of the ground. The soft white petals loomed across the huge field, engulfing the whole of it. From the petals came new sprouts, which grew into children, which then grew into adults, and they were all playing football.

"Football!" I said, as I shot up from the couch, waking from my dream. And I knew what to do with my shop.

Chapter Eight

I rose the following morning encouraged, happy with the direction my plans had taken, or I guess, that I had plans at all.

The frosted morning grass made a crunching sound as I walked across the field between Jack's house and my lot. I visualized my little shop as I stood next to my tiny little sprout. I would set up the Kingdom's very first footballer's shop, I proudly thought to myself. I would make and sell footballs. I wasn't sure *how* of course; I didn't even know what kind of plant was growing in the back of my lot, but I was pretty well certain it wasn't a *leather* tree.

And I frowned at the deduction that real rawhide leather was out of the question, as there weren't any animals in the Kingdom, at least none that I'd seen. And even though I remembered Little Miss Charity and the Shepherd having made mention several times of *sheep*, I'll admit, I had no idea what they were talking about.

Either way, football seemed to be the one thing this kingdom was missing, and I was sure the good people of this magical, yet sheltered constituency would eventually come to thank me for introducing it. Just like my dream, I could picture people coming from all over the Kingdom to the field behind my lot, hundreds even, just to be together and play or watch some friendly competition.

I could even teach them, I thought, tossing the idea back and forth in my head. I could host clinics, like *Foot Control with Branan*, or *Minimizing Your Penalty Area*. Maybe not...

Having a solidified visionary directive, I could now begin setting up shop. I wasn't sure how fast things would grow in the Kingdom, but I was certain to have at least days, if not weeks or months before my plant would be anywhere near harvestable.

I of course hoped it would grow into something useful to my directive, but regardless of what my plant was, I didn't care if it was a bloody *cabbage*; I was determined to figure out some way of using it to help me make footballs. So, with that settled, I could begin setting up my shop now, while I waited.

I stood calculating, scaling sizes up and down in my mind, thinking about how my shop might look. About that time, I felt the awareness of someone approaching from behind me.

"How's it coming?" asked Cassia, as I turned to meet her smile. She blushed slightly at my expression, as it was obvious I enjoyed looking at her. "What?" she smiled as I stood wordless.

"Nothing," I smiled back, feeling slightly stupid. "You just, look... good- nice, I mean, you look nice."

"Stop that, would you," she answered, though her smile had brightened even more. Apparently she was growing at least a little more comfortable with my positive opinion of her.

"You just don't know how to respond to compliments," I added awkwardly, smiling back.

"Aye, is that it?" she rolled her eyes, blushing. "Good work,

Detective."

"Come look at this," I changed the subject, motioning to my little sprout. "Tell me what you think this is going to be."

Stepping up to the little, blossoming bud, she examined it as though she knew what to look for in answering inquiries of the botanical nature.

"Going to be?" she repeated. "I think you should say *is*."

"Well, aye, but it's not much yet."

"It's enough to tell what it is."

"What is it?"

"Well, I can't be certain; I don't have any of my books handy, but it looks like a-"

"Your books?"

"Aye. In Perth, I was studying Botany."

"Were you?"

"Aye. I've always been fascinated by the growth of all things from something so small as a seed."

"...Ironic."

"Aye?"

"Well, it's just, I would say you came to the right place then."

She smiled, then turned her gaze to the horizon, "Da says *everyone* eventually finds that his passions make sense in the Kingdom..."

Now understand, I respected Jack's opinion very much, but I didn't want to bother with processing the thoughts they evoked. And as his daughter spoke his words, I could tell she was more thinking aloud than stating her belief, so I allowed a moment of pause for her uncertainty.

"...I interrupted you," I said, once I saw her eyes had shifted back toward the here and now.

"What?"

"You started to tell me the name of the-"

"Oh, right. I was going to say, it looks like it may be Ficus Elastica."

"What's *Ficus Elastica*?"

"Most call it *Rubber Plant*. It grows to be about this wide," she stretched out her arms, "about this tall, and it has big, thick, wide, leathery leaves-"

"Wait, really?" I interrupted, turning to face her.

"...Aye," she answered with a questioning look. "Is that alright...?"

"It's perfect!" I beamed. "I was wondering what to use for the- See, I want to open the Kingdom's first footballer's shop. These leaves you speak of could be dried and oiled and used for the skin of the-" I was excited now, blabbering at the speed of sound. "I want to make and sell footballs, understand. And this nice field behind my lot could be used for a playing field, with the permission of your family of course. This kingdom could use a little more sport, I think."

She tilted her head just a bit to one side, a little surprised by either the idea itself or my excitement of it. "That's actually a really good idea-"

"Do you want to go in with me on this?" I interrupted again.

"You mean like, help tend your shop?"

"No, I mean you and I both tend *our* shop."

"You mean we share the profits?"

"Aye."

"Mind you, that's a fine offer, but I'm not sure I could."

"And why is this?" I asked. This confused me. Who wouldn't want to make money?

"Well, you know my commitments at home."

"Aye, and I could help you with those."

"You would do that?"

"Aye. I'd help you with your chores, and you'd help me tend my shop."

"You mean *our* shop," she corrected with a smile.

"Aye," I laughed.

And indeed it was. We spent the next several days excitedly making plans for our shop, and she put in just as much as I did. We worked out the schedule of our day so that we'd be able to divide the housework evenly between us and have enough time left over to work the shop and make a profit. Mind you, we weren't working the shop *yet* though, we had yet to build it.

And as to that, we came up with some great ideas. We decided not to begin building until the Rubber Plant was harvestable, but eagerly awaited that day.

I met up with Gunty and asked if he knew anyone who had access to woodworking supplies and equipment. He introduced me to a huge man, about the size of himself, by the name of Hamish.

Hamish offered to use good, solid wood, but nothing too special, so as to afford us a very good price for building our shop. He even offered free of charge to carve an ornate heading above the counter, to which we heartily accepted.

We were enjoying the excitement of beginning something new, and at the same time, we were enjoying spending time together.

Cassia quickly became special to me, and I was looking for all the little things, like trying to find excuses to brush shoulders, or "accidentally" touch her hand while we worked. When these things happened, I noticed how her body seemed to tense, or her face would blush slightly, or she would draw a quick, almost silent breath in.

Or that tiny, almost unnoticeable reaction she had to my voice when we worked very closely together in tight quarters, I looked for that as well.

It was becoming obvious, even to others, that there was a mutual interest. We would go for walks down the stone avenue, and people would look at us. I'd see wives nudge their husbands and smile, whispering things like, "Ah, young love..."

Or we'd go to the loch, if we weren't terribly busy, just to breathe in the breeze off the water, and we both knew the other was thinking the same. That was just it: we both knew, and yet nothing was done or said about it. Perhaps that was the fun of it.

"What are we?" she finally asked me one day as we sat in the grass by the loch.

It was so abrupt; I didn't catch it at first. "…We're people. We're Scottish. We're adults. We're intelligent-"

"You know what I mean," she interrupted with a smile and a nudge.

"No, really," I smiled back, "what *do* you mean?"

"I mean, what are we?" she repeated. "Are we *friends*? Am I your *girlfriend*? What's our," she paused, "what's our *status*, no?"

"*Status…*" I repeated the word soberly, half smiling. "I didn't realize we had to have one."

"Well… I'd like to know, I guess…"

I didn't really know what to say. I was unprepared for the thought. On one hand, I definitely thought of her as my girlfriend, and no mistake. But on the other, I was in a place called *the Kingdom*, a strange, magical, uncertain place I didn't truly belong, a place I was never really certain was even real, a place she never intended to leave.

Sure, I'd kept myself busy with the shop and all, but that had just sort of *come upon me*, as it were. Underneath it all, I'd never even planned on being here this long in the first place. As far as I knew, my brother and I were on the first train out. I wasn't even sure why we hadn't left yet.

So I told her the only thing I knew about us for certain, "I'm Branan and you're Cassia. I guess I hadn't really gotten much past that."

"Oh."

I realized by her eyes that my answer had come out a little

more rigid than I meant it.

"I mean, don't get me wrong," I quickly added, to soften my previous words. "I enjoy being with you, whether we're working or talking or whatever. -And you're certainly the prettiest girl I know. I just hadn't really… thought about…" I sort of trailed off before adding, "Is it necessary that we have a *status*?"

"I suppose not," she said, and then added a sheepish smile and glance, "as long as you've not made plans to go anywhere for awhile."

"I've not made plans past an hour or so since I arrived," I smiled back. "Right now, my only real plans are to set up this shop with you and work at it for as long as… whenever."

"I suppose that'll do for now," she smiled, half-heartedly.

And so things between Cassia and I stayed pretty much as they were, and we kept focused on our shop, as though it were the project that mattered above all else.

It wasn't long before the Rubber Plant was harvestable, and from there it seemed no time at all before all the pieces fell into place and the shop was up and running.

Surprisingly enough, interest grew fast, as though the Kingdom were quite ripe for the Beautiful Game; it seemed there was a general intrigue. We couldn't make footballs fast enough, even though most of the purchasers didn't really know much about how to use them.

As it turned out, I did have to host clinics, as I'd proposed I might, so that the interested parties could learn the game. I formed several teams and officiated their games. Of course it was quite some time before the games became even remotely exciting; Cassia, Tommy, and myself being the only three who were any good, the field resembled something of a circus performance. But when all was said and done, I saw fit to form the *Leather Leaf Football Club*; which had to be done after so many teams had formed. The field was properly painted, goals were made and fixed to the ground at each end, and Hamish, once I explained to him the concept of bleachers, built some nice, wooden ones.

I'd *imagined* it could be just so, that so many would rally to the game just like in the dream I'd had, but never *truly* thought it would happen. In what seemed like a flash, I had set up and become king of a football empire. I'd have been overwhelmed, had it not come together so naturally, so easily.

I only wished my brother could've been there with me. No one loved and respected the Beautiful Game like him. To work with him side by side, to see him and Crystal grow closer together, as I assumed they were, to see his approval of my interest in Cassia, all these things would have made my accomplishments more complete somehow.

But I *didn't* see him. Day after day passed, and still no sign of Drostan. I of course assumed he and Crystal were still with the Shepherd, though I had no real way of knowing. I tried not to think much about it, or at least, not to let it bother me, and continued to focus all my attention on building up Leather Leaf.

After several weeks, it must have been, there were enough

talented, athletic people properly trained that we could divide the teams into divisions with separate officials for each game. This way, I could focus on coaching instead of having to police the field.

As our first official season got underway, it was quite obvious that I'd been right: football was precisely what this place had been missing. The footballers, those who fell in love with the game and had no shop to attend, would train with Cassia, Tommy, and me throughout the day to shape up their skills. Then, once the avenue shops had been closed down for the day, people came from every corner of the Kingdom to watch as the games began.

I enjoyed many games from the sidelines, coaching opposite Cassia or Tommy, but one stands out. The memory has nothing to do with football really, but it was on the day of this particular game I speak of that my eyes were opened to the beginning of an understanding that changed my life forever.

Chapter Nine

It was a nice day, I remember that much; a clear sky, not too sunny, not too rainy, perfect for football. It was sometime after the half; we were up one goal and had been for some time, but Tommy's team just wouldn't come off it.

I remember; I'd called a timeout for a sort of pep talk, or whatever I could muster to ensure my lads keep our advantage. I'd advised Kevin, our goalkeeper, to mind the leftfield striker; Kevin had been a little careless with the right side of the net and was fortunate that it hadn't cost us as of yet.

I was nearly through with my *excellent work on stopping the rightfield wingman's cross* speech to the fullbacks, when I noticed a familiar stride at the sideline across the field. It was my brother; he and Crystal were walking hand in hand, having come to watch a game, I'd supposed.

It felt strange seeing him, like that feeling when you walk back through your door after having been on holiday for a long time. But what struck me as more strange was the look he had, he and Crystal both. They looked somehow different than they had before, though I didn't know what it was.

From then, my mind was elsewhere, as I waited anxiously for the end of the game, having lost any real desire for the *glorious victory*. I was eager to speak with them. But, once the game had ended, I couldn't find them. In the bustle of people coming and going from the field, I suppose they'd slipped away without my having noticed.

I was disappointed not to have spoken with them, but then I saw them once more at the game the following evening and again at the next, neither time catching up to them before they left. Fearing they may be purposefully avoiding my company, though I admit I had no real grounds for such a theory, I sat out from coaching one evening so that I might follow them once they left.

I felt foolish and deceitful standing to the back corner of the bleachers so as to be hidden from my brother, but I did it all the same, watching and waiting.

Not long before the end of the game, I saw them stand from their seats to leave, and so I followed cautiously. I trailed them from far enough a distance so as to not be noticed, as they walked through the neighborhood surrounding the football field, and then into the Pine Grove. Once in the dense grove, I shortened the distance between them and myself a bit, safely hidden in the trees.

As I followed, I assumed the destination was the Shepherd's Garden, and I wondered how I'd be received. If the Shepherd saw me, what would he say? Equally, why did I care? Why was it that this Shepherd's disposition toward me mattered?

The Shepherd made me feel something in the center of myself that I couldn't explain. It was as though there were something about him deeper than I understood. I couldn't answer *why* these things were important to me; I just knew they were.

My discomfort with these uncertainties is the reason I turned around and went back. As I walked, toeing fallen twigs and little mounds of dirt on the ground, I pictured Drostan and Crystal. What was it about them that I had noticed? Something was different; I just couldn't isolate it in my mind.

I pictured the look on Crystals face, that look my eyes had caught a few days ago, even from across the field, the look that was mirrored the same on Drostan's face. I assumed they had fallen in love; all the signs showed it, but there was something besides. The only phrase I could think of to describe what I saw in their eyes was *inner peace...*

Then it hit me. They had found contentment.

Here, here in this kingdom, everything had seemed temporary to me. Everything was a diversion, without permanence, to keep me occupied. It wasn't the same for them. I felt I knew that with certainty. They had found true contentment to stay in the Shepherd's Garden, not merely to live *as though the diversions of living were the highest purpose*, as Jack had said.

But that's *exactly* what *I* was doing. I was wasting time. And I was wasting Cassia's time.

By the time I got back to the field, it was all but empty; only one person remained. Cassia stood at the sidelines, near the bleachers.

"Where you been?" she asked.

"Walking."

"You look like a man with a lot on his mind."

"Mmm," I mumbled noncommittally.

"I'm a good listener," she tugged each earlobe with a wink.

I took a deep breath in, betraying the gravity of my thoughts.

"We should go our separate ways I think."

She paused for a long moment before answering with a flat smile that told me she'd been thinking similar thoughts, "We're mostly wasting each other's time, no?"

"Aye," I shrugged with the same flat smile to affirm that we were on the same page.

"You know, Branan, that I care for you very deeply-"

"And I you," I interrupted.

We reached silently to each other, and she set her soft, precious hands in mine. I pulled her to me, placing her head against my chest in a gentle embrace.

"But I feel that I should go."

"Where will you go?" she whispered.

"The Shepherd's Garden."

"But he's the…" She looked for the words. "He's the *Shepherd*. Wouldn't that be imposing?"

"I don't think so. I don't know how to explain, but I feel like… I feel like that's what he *wants*, for us all to be his friends. I think that's the meaning of this whole place."

"Maybe…" She wasn't convinced, but I didn't need her to be. I hated to leave her behind, but I'd made my decision.

"Either way, I'm leaving."

She paused, "When?"

"Uh, now, actually."

She lifted the side of her face from my chest, replacing it with her hands in front of her, looking me in the eyes with a single tear stream trailing down her face. It was only then that I realized she had begun to cry somewhere in our discourse. My heart squeezed.

"But what about our shop?" she asked, sounding, for the first time during the conversation, a little hurt.

"We have a great shop," I answered with a smile, "And we *have* provided the people of this kingdom with a positive entertainment, but this has all been merely a diversion for me. I didn't realize it until now; it seemed like so much more, being with you, tending the shop, bringing footballers together in friendly competition; but I've just been wasting time, avoiding what I knew was important. I need to leave it... I thought I'd turn the shop over to you and Tommy."

"...Alright..."

I paused for a moment, worried that I'd caused irreparable damage, and so I finally came out with the truth.

"I- I *do* love you."

She looked deep into my eyes, with a mix of what almost seemed like shock (though I was sure she knew this truth), and hope.

After a moment, she whispered back, "And I you. You know this."

"Aye."

"So why must you go?"

How in the world could I tell her everything that was in my heart? "I can't explain. But I do plan to see you again."

This didn't seem to provide much comfort, but I knew nothing better to say. So I held her face in my hands, kissed her lips softly, turned, and walked away.

I was nervous as I walked along the great, stone wall around the Kingdom. I was worried about the Diggers and the Tree Sprites. The one other time I'd been here, the Shepherd was with me. I wondered what would be done to me now that I was alone with no protection.

All the same, I was glad to be alone. I didn't want to talk to anyone. I wanted to be free to think as I walked.

After a long breath in, I mustered up the courage and stepped forward from the Back Meadow into the Drylands. I scanned the horizon for danger and noticed the Shepherd in step beside me.

"Oh," I startled, "I didn't see you there."

He chuckled a little. "I thought you might prefer an escort. And don't worry; I know you're not in the mood to talk." He mimicked the locking of his mouth.

"Aye, and thank you."

He nodded.

We walked in silence all the way through the Drylands and up the forested mountainside. As we walked, I thought about this strange man. I suppose I considered him a friend, but why? Just because he was kind? He'd invited me into his Kingdom, to his special garden; he'd even given me a seed to produce wealth for myself. Was that it, his power? His wealth? He owned his own Kingdom. I'd never known anyone like that. Did I just want to associate with him for my own gain? I felt that I'd left Cassia to be near him for more noble a reason than selfish gain, but I wasn't sure what it was.

Once I'd reached the secret door, I turned to speak with the Shepherd, only to realize he was no longer with me. Just as he'd appeared beside me before the Drylands, it was as though he'd vanished with the breeze.

I shook my head to clear it and entered the narrow alley.

Stepping in under the canopy, I took in the waft of sweet, organic scent that hit my face. Suddenly, I couldn't help but feel calm; a strange sense of peace I didn't quite understand swept over me in that instant and I knew I had made the right decision to return here.

Glancing down to the clover and moss between my shoes, it occurred to me that I'd never really appreciated the beauty of such simple things before. How much had I missed out on, *living as though the diversions of living were the highest purpose*? Had I never truly seen the beauty of Golspie, Portree, Snowdon, the Shannon Basin, or *any* of the haunts I'd held in high regard?

Staring down in thought as I was, trying to decide what to think or say or ask or do, I heard a twig snap underfoot and looked up to see Drostan coming toward me with a smile.

"How goes it?" he asked with the awkwardness that comes when friends, brothers as close as us have not spoken for a long time.

"...Just trying to make sense of things, Dros. You?"

"We're quite well, thank you."

I couldn't help but notice the "*we*," so I asked with a grin, "You love her, don't you?"

"Aye," he smiled back, and I saw that he meant it. Behind his eyes, I saw that look again, that look of peace and contentment.

"Crystal and I are going to stay," he added after a moment.

I stared in his eyes, thinking about what all that meant, not knowing what to say...

"What's it like?" I finally asked.

"Come for a walk with me."

Without a word between us, I followed my brother deeper into the garden, stopping behind him once we were in the thick of the ferns.

He turned to face me, "I'm glad you came, Branan." He spoke with such fervor and sincerity.

It was then that I realized why I'd recognized the look on Drostan's face; he looked like the Shepherd. That look in the Shepherd's eyes that made anywhere feel like home, that's what I felt now, talking with Drostan.

"What's happened to you?" I asked. "You seem so..." I couldn't find the right word.

"Full?" he supplied for me.

"Something. I- I can't name it..."

"It's..." he paused to find the words. "It's being here. It's finding a place, a *real place* inside of everything."

"I don't understand, mate...?"

"It's all this life that never stops growing; it's the Shepherd; it's Crystal," and as he spoke, Crystal slid down a vine from somewhere up in the canopy and placed her hand into his with a smile to me, and I saw home in her eyes as well. She was so beautiful; it was hard to believe that this was the same frail, bony, dying girl we'd found on the streets of Exploit.

"It's joining together," Drostan continued, "uniting life to plant the seeds we've been given and grow them together into something new and beautiful."

"Well spoken," said a voice from behind me. "It's the *reason* for the garden."

I turned and faced the Shepherd to find him smiling, "*My* garden, which is the reason for the Kingdom."

"Shepherd," began Drostan, "may we share The Cocoon with others?"

An even broader smile spread across the Shepherd's face, "It pleases me that you would ask, for this is the reason that such sacred things exist, to be shared. Only, be sure to keep it sacred. Never offer pearls to pigs."

Drostan nodded. "It will only be Branan for the present, of course."

"I find this very agreeable, my son."

"Thank you, Shepherd," said Drostan with a nod. I followed suit with a cordial nod to the same, having no idea what was going on, and I saw my brother and Crystal turn to leave. I followed, not knowing what else to do.

The Cocoon... I tried not to process the thought; merely trusting my brother and following behind.

As we walked through the ferns and deep into a thick grove of cane and ivy, they explained.

"So here's how it happened," Drostan began. "We both decided to plant our seeds in the Shepherd's Garden-"

"It just seemed to make sense," Crystal interrupted.

"Aye," Drostan agreed, "there's so much growing here anyway. It's a healthy environment, understand."

"Quite," she agreed, looking at him as he looked lovingly back at her, and I wondered if they remembered they were talking to me.

"So mine grew to be not but a wee bit of ivy," he continued.

"Silverking," Crystal expounded. "Pretty, but-"

"Not worth the space it occupies," he shrugged.

"And mine grew to be a tiny spruce, less than a foot or so from his ivy. It wasn't a conscious thing, planting our seeds next to each other, we just *happened* to."

"But it *became* important," Drostan modified. "Coming everyday to tend our plants, side by side, we began to realize we had more than infatuation." He put his arm around her as he said it.

"No pretenses, we just fell in love, full stop." As she spoke, she gazed at him adoringly. *His* eyes, however, never left mine; I could see that he was intending to communicate something to me in this story, something he held in high importance.

My brother continued, in a slightly more sober tone, "And it sounds crazy, but as we grew closer together, so did our plants."

"We had chosen to share life," Crystal added, "a covenant like, forever united."

"And once it was decided," Drostan continued with a smile, "the ivy began to twine around the wee trunk of the spruce. The two began to grow together."

"And they grew like fire," Crystal added, her eyes sparkling. "It was like, once they were together, they grew toward a purpose."

"Within a few weeks, we came to find this."

He raised his hand up to direct my eyes to the object of our walk through the growth. I followed his arm up to see a huge, organic ball some twenty feet above ground. It was probably about the size of a large drawing room, supported at the bottom by a wide trunk wrapped in thick, silver ivy, both of which ran enormous, thirsty roots into the ground.

"*The Cocoon?*"

"Aye," he answered with a bright smile. "Let me show you."

He hoisted Crystal up first and then followed her, climbing up the ivy-wrapped trunk like a ladder. I followed, still not having fully processed the scene.

Upon reaching the base of The Cocoon itself, I followed my brother through a hole just big enough to barely fit. Once inside, I gasped in surprise, looking up to see an impossibly big, open sky. Being far more vast here on the inside, I knew it must be the

Shepherd's magic that made this place possible.

Under the huge, beautiful, blue canopy, I saw a vast expanse of green. The grasses sprinkled here and there with a touch of color, flowers of all kinds. It seemed to go on forever in every direction.

"We call it The Cocoon because of the outside," said Crystal. "But I suppose it would be more appropriately called a meadow. As you can see, that's what we have here."

"Isn't it gorgeous?" asked Drostan.

"Aye," I answered, still wide-eyed, "it is that indeed."

"It's like we have our own little world inside the Shepherd's Garden," Crystal beamed.

Then I began to understand.

Over the last, well, however long it had been, I had done the same with my seed as I had in relation to Cassia; I had worked hard to create something nice for myself.

And my seed had done well, well at least *alright*. It had produced a Rubber Plant, which I had used, to the best of my knowledge and ability, to accomplish the goal I had set for myself. As a matter of fact, I got a lot from my seed, as per its potential.

But my brother's seed had served to create a whole new *world*. Was this simply about love?

"This happened because of your love for one another?"

"Aye," he answered, "oh, but not that *alone*," he hurried to qualify. "The growth of our seeds took time; we haven't told you anything about that *time between*."

"Aye," I said, just now remembering their long absence. "I

haven't seen you for weeks. What happened?"

"We've stayed here with the Shepherd, gotten to know him. He's a very wise man; I've learned a lot from him. And I've come to love him like family."

"What's that got to do with all this," I waved my hand to the grandeur of the meadow around me.

"Everything. *Life* is what causes a seed to grow to its full potential. And the life of anything is in its source, no?"

"Aye."

"The *Shepherd* is the source of the seeds."

I struggled to comprehend, "So you're saying the Shepherd makes the seeds *magical*?"

"Well…" he struggled for the right words, "more *brings the seeds to their full potential.*"

"But this Cocoon is like a whole 'nother *world*!"

"Aye," he said, gazing around, obviously still in wonder of it all himself.

It still wasn't fitting together for me. "How can being near someone cause a plant to grow into another world?"

"Mmm," he shrugged. "How can being near Cassia cause you to turn a tiny footballer's shop into a kingdom-wide football club?"

I paused for a moment to think. "I suppose my love for her- working with her- towards an ambition- maybe, to win her heart, I suppose. I suppose that made it possible."

I pondered that a moment. It was true. Without my having loved Cassia and wanting to prove myself and be the man she needed, I would have accomplished much less.

"Aye," he affirmed. "It was possible because authentic love is as good as *magic*."

"Point taken."

"A seed from the Shepherd is kind of like that I should think."

"Like love you mean?"

"Aye. Coming from its source and with somewhere to grow to," he smiled, "there's no stopping it." Then he simply shrugged, turned on his heels, and continued in the direction we'd come thus far.

Chapter Ten

I'm sure it must've been at least a mile we'd walked before I noticed we were approaching a little cabin. I hadn't paid much attention as to where we were going; my eyes had been occupied with the grandeur of the meadow that surrounded us.

We'd walked by a small loch with cattails and reeds, whistling woodwinds who sang to us as we passed them by. We crossed a babbling brook, which refracted the soft light, reflecting off the sparkling stones beneath. We climbed a subtle knoll whose long, feathery grasses bowed to us in the light breeze.

It wasn't until we'd crested the second hill past a huge, gorgeous patch of silverking that the cabin came into view.

It wasn't but a wee cottage, constructed of logs, with a stone chimney atop it. Thick, white smoke puffed from the chimney and everything about the place said, "Stop in for a biscuit."

"What's this?" I asked, nodding toward the cabin. "Someone live there?"

"Hice Numa," my brother answered.

"Who?" I wondered if I'd heard correctly.

"I know, it's a strange name, but that's how he introduced himself to me. What's even weirder; he looked just like me, a reflection in a mirror-"

"But she looked like me too," interrupted Crystal.

"She?"

"Yeah, to me."

"That's crazy," I suggested.

"Aye, that's why I wanted to bring you here. You need to meet him- er- You need to meet Hice Numa. It's an *experience*, brother, no mistake." And then he looked at Crystal with a smile, still speaking to me, "What he has to show you, well, it'll change you, mate."

From the looks in their eyes, I gathered for the first time what they had intended all along. Their showing me this meadow had really been all about my meeting the person in this cabin. All else was secondary.

The gravity of the situation, as well as Drostan's statement presented a bit of an awkward pause, giving me a moment to consider whatever this time might hold. Then, with a little grin and shrug to affirm that all was as it should be, my brother led us down the hill toward the cabin.

Stepping into the yard as it seemed to be, though it had no other boundary to separate it from the grass of the rest of the meadow; I noticed that *this* grass was just a bit greener, slightly plusher. But I couldn't focus on this long; for some reason, I was on edge. We stepped up onto the narrow, little front porch and Drostan reached up to knock on the door. Just as I probably could have predicted, the little, rickety door creaked open before Drostan had a chance to knock.

"Welcome!" said happily the man who could only have been

Hice Numa.

A feeling came over me that I've no explanation for; it *was* just like looking in a mirror. I stared for a moment, seeing the same stare returned, except that there was a smile in my reflection, and the Shepherd's eyes in place of my own.

"I'm Branan," I said mindlessly, robotically reaching out my hand. He took it in his with a firm shake. I felt all and nothing in that handshake. On the one hand, it felt as though when our hands met my whole life flashed and was judged within a single moment. On the other hand, it was obvious from his eyes that he was ready and willing to accept me just as I was, with no bias.

"May I have a few moments?" he asked my company.

"Of course," answered Drostan with a smile, and the two stepped down from the porch. As I watched them walk away, I felt a bit of panic concerning my awkwardness in this situation. How was I supposed to act? I didn't know what to say to this person. Hopefully he'd do most of the talking.

"I'm sure you must be feeling uncomfortable," he said once I'd turned back to him.

"This, this is all new to me," I stuttered.

"As well it should be. It is to everyone. Every time." He smiled reassurance.

"Other people come here?"

"Well, not exactly *here*. This place is sacred to Drostan and his Crystal. Everyone has his own safe place; I'm only meeting you here because *yours* happens to be with your brother."

"Is that bad?" I asked. I had no idea what the protocol was.

"Not bad," my reflection smiled, "just, *temporary.*"

"So," I didn't know what to say.

Thankfully, he took the floor once again, "I wanted to speak with you alone, just as I did with your brother and his companion, to explain who I am. But first, I want you to know why it matters."

I stood, simply staring, wearing my questions all over my face.

"The Shepherd gave you a seed, no?"

"Aye."

"You consulted him concerning the care of it, no?"

"No," I answered after a moment, chagrined. Even as he said it, the obviousness of it slapped me in the face. Why hadn't I done this?

"Indeed," he smiled flatly. "Understand, I've no intention of shaming you. I'm merely displaying the facts."

"Aye," I confirmed.

"So, you nurtured your seed by your own means, to your own ends, no?"

"Aye."

"Your results were somewhat profitable, no?"

"Somewhat."

"So, what's the lot of it?"

"Well," I considered the question, "what do you mean?"

"It seems you're alright on your own, no? So why did you leave your Cassia?"

I paused to think. "I suppose... because... I can't expect to make her happy... if I feel like I'm missing something."

"Exactly. So what are you missing?"

"I'm not sure, but I think Drostan has it. That's why I came here."

"And now we're back to square one: who I am."

Still confused, still distracted by thoughts of Cassia, I couldn't get the picture of her face out of my head, not that I wanted to. Her beautiful face, those big pretty eyes full of questions...

I continued to try to focus on Hice Numa's every word and somehow draw out the meaning. I had the feeling that this man was like the Shepherd, in that everything he said would mean something deeper than the words themselves.

"When you look at me, you see yourself, no? It's because I'm a type of you."

"A *type* of me?" I asked.

"An *image* of you, sort of like a shadow, but reversed."

"What do you mean?"

"A shadow follows after; I've come *before* you, to show you who you could be, who you *can* be if you choose."

"What do you mean, 'who I can be'? Who can I be?"

"Me."

"But I still don't know who you are."

He stared even more intently into my eyes. "I think you do."

Beginning to become slightly impatient with his riddles, I said, "I don't mean to be rude, Sir, but I feel like I'm becoming less intelligent the longer we talk."

A small snicker, not unkind but full of humor, escaped his lips. "I'm sorry, I shouldn't have a laugh at your expense. And I *am* sorry to confuse or frustrate you, I don't intend to; I just know the importance of your coming to the answer yourself."

Giving him the benefit of the doubt, I submitted to the situation before me and tried to talk my way through his little equation, "So, you look like my 'reverse shadow'," I said falling back on his terminology, "*identical*, as far as I can tell."

"Identical?" he questioned.

"Well, all but your eyes."

Again, he looked as excited as a mother whose child just said his first word. "Which are the window in."

"*In?*"

"To the soul, the core of a person," he explained. Then after a short pause, he asked, "So how do my eyes differ?" I could tell he was trying to lead me somewhere.

I thought a moment, before finally answering, "In your eyes, strangely, I see the Shepherd, just like my brother and his girlfriend."

"Aye, but why would that be?" Again, he was leading me.

"Why would *what* be?" I asked, throwing up my hands in frustration. "I'm not pretending to understand *any* of this."

"It would help you to stop letting that stand in your way."

I felt as if I were getting one condescending riddle after another, and wondered if maybe I should've never left Cassia in the first place.

He continued, returning back to his question, "Why would it be that, from the outside, I should be *you* by all appearances, when from the inside looking out, I should be the Shepherd?"

I finally exploded, "I have no bloody idea! That's what I'm saying!"

His flat smile remained, with a slight tone of irritation in his voice, "It *is* easier to fall back on that, isn't it?"

I paused for a short moment at what seemed to me like audacity, "Come again?"

"Just think, brother; *think*. I've given you all the pieces. Telling yourself you don't understand won't help you to. You can't begin to see anything in a puzzle until you start putting the pieces together."

"Okay, I'll try," I said as more acquiescence to an impasse than a willing compliance.

I finally said, "I guess it's like... it's like you're a blend of me and the Shepherd. I know that doesn't make any sense; that's just the best I can come up with."

"Why does that not make any sense?" he asked, in a tone that implied it was the most reasonable thing in the world.

"Because it's stupid," I said, still annoyed to be treated like a child. "What would be the point of me coming to a random log cabin in a magical meadow to have a conversation with myself as the Shepherd? See, I even sounded daft saying it."

"You're so worried about what might not make sense," he said in a calm tone. "Personally, I think it makes *perfect* sense."

"How is that?" I retorted.

"Think about what you told your Cassia; quote, 'I feel like that's what he *wants*, for us all to be his friends. I think that's the meaning of this whole place.' Have you thought about the possibility that you're right?"

It should have shocked me, I suppose, that he could quote me verbatim, not having been there for the conversation, but I suppose I'd gotten used to the magic of this place. I remembered that conversation with specificity. I remembered the look in her eyes when I told her I was leaving. I remember wishing she would come with me.

"I *do* think I'm right," I finally said, calming myself a bit, "but what's that have to do with this?"

"Everything. Why do you think the Shepherd would want his sheep to be his friends?"

This reminded me of the question I'd had ever since my brother and I had arrived, "That's another thing I don't get; why do I keep hearing people being called sheep?"

He didn't answer at first. "I'll let you figure that one out on your own," he finally said with a knowing smile, before routing me back, "Why would the Shepherd want his sheep to be his friends?"

"I suppose because he cares about us," I threw out.

"This whole kingdom is his," he added. "Only *he* can truly make sense of it."

"And if we're to be here with him," I spoke in pieces, as it were, "then I suppose," letting each piece hang so I may hear it myself, "he'd want *us* all to make sense of it?"

"Aye," he said emphatically.

It was starting to come together in my head. Drostan and Crystal really did seem to feel at home here. It's like they'd made sense of it, just like Hice Numa was saying. They'd submitted to being the Shepherd's sheep; not just to take advantage of the Kingdom's benefits, like most of the shop owners. Instead, they had truly, consciously chosen to love him and treat him like a real friend. That was the difference; I hadn't done that.

"I'm merely what you could be if you'd choose to plant your seed in the Shepherd's Garden," continued Hice Numa. "The life that shines out his eyes would be the same in yours."

I focused on the Shepherd's eyes in my reflection until the Shepherd was all I saw before me. I addressed whom I saw there, "Shepherd."

"Son?"

I spoke the only words I could possibly think to say at that moment, "I'm sorry for taking lightly your gift. You gave me a seed and I used it for my own ends. Can you forgive me?"

A smile spread across the Shepherd's face as a tear rolled down his cheek. "It makes me happy to."

"Is there any way you can give me another chance?" I asked hesitantly.

Without a word, he reached into his pouch and pulled from it a plush, green seed. He held it out to me, looking me in the eyes.

I took it from his hand with gravity, "Thank you, Shepherd. I'll plant this one in your garden, I promise."

"I think you'll come to find that it's the only way to make sense of it."

"Of what?" I asked, slightly confused.

"Planting, growing, harvesting."

Understanding came. "Is that why you chose this place?"

"What do you mean?"

"I mean, is this place more fertile, this plot of land? Is that why you chose to plant your garden here?"

"Oh, no son. You've got it backwards," he smiled. "The plot became fertile because I chose to plant here."

I had to take a moment to register that. This man had even more power than I'd imagined.

"So, was it barren when you first arrived?"

"Aye."

An interesting thought came to me, "What did you plant first?"

He paused just a moment. "My word," he said.

That wasn't what I expected. I was waiting for an answer like corn, or peas, or cotton. "What?" I asked.

He smiled at me in my confusion. "I'm sure you've noticed the magic of this place."

I grinned at the understanding. "To say the least, Sir," I said with a slight laugh.

"Aye," he smiled, "and the magic comes from me."

"I thought as much," I affirmed respectfully.

"I spoke Life into the ground and it became as I'd said."

I stared at him in wonder. "What exactly does that mean?"

"To speak Life?"

"Aye."

"One day you'll understand fully, but for now, the best example I can give is affirmation."

"Affirmation?"

"When you speak affirming words, even simple things, like when you tell Drostan that he's a talented footballer for example, you are speaking life."

"But isn't that different? I mean, I can't *create life* by speaking, like you do."

He raised his eyebrows with a grin. "Are you sure about that?"

I furrowed my brow in confusion.

"This cocoon," he said, motioning to the plush beauty around us, "sprang up from three small words of life."

"I thought it grew from two seeds."

Here, he seemed to get excited again, "But the full potential of the seeds came from the union of your brother and his Crystal. That union couldn't have begun without the words '*I love you.*' Very strong words of Life, those," he ended seriously.

I thought on these things, half *in* the moment, half somewhere else altogether, and my thoughts naturally led to Cassia.

"Shepherd," I thought aloud, "I don't know what to do." I didn't clarify what I meant, but he of course knew anyway.

"About your Cassia," he perceived.

"Aye. I want to stay here with you, to live in your garden; my heart is *here* now, but I've left a piece of it with Cassia. I don't want to leave here and go back, but I don't want to leave her either." All the pain and confusion I was feeling came out in my voice.

He paused to let me soak in the moment before asking, "Can you live without your Cassia?"

I paused as well, at the gravity of the question. "I'm not sure I can, Sir," I finally answered.

"Sometimes lad, you have to risk losing something you love to attain that which you can't live without." He paused with a deep breath in. "Let me tell you a story..."

Here my father stopped his story, still looking at me with a slight smile, as if he were pondering whether or not to continue.

"Well...?" I asked, my fingers wrapped tight around the top of my blanket, as I had spent the past hour or so, totally engrossed in my father's fairytale.

Still nothing.

"Are you going to finish the story, Dad?"

"Aye, but... I think I should save the Shepherd's story for when you're a bit older."

"Awe, come on Dad," I groaned.

"Nah, I think I should wait. It's a very sad story and I don't want to upset you. I'll tell you someday when you're older, I promise. Now, where was I?"

I was still disappointed, but badly wanted to hear the rest of the story. "You were talking to the Shepherd in Uncle Drostan's cocoon."

"Aye, and so the Shepherd said I should ask Cassia to come live in his garden with us. I hadn't thought about that; maybe I *didn't* have to choose between the Shepherd's Garden and Cassia after all. Maybe these two pieces of my heart could coexist.

"But I was nervous about facing Cassia and her family with the idea of taking her away from them. But when I pictured the happiness in her beautiful eyes to see me at her door, I decided the risk was worth it."

"Is that when you asked Grandpa Jack if you could marry Mom?"

"Don't say it *aloud*, lass," my father whispered. "You'll ruin the story."

I hid a smile, mimicking the locking shut of my mouth to let him continue.

"And so I went to the home of Jack the plow smith and I asked his daughter if she would come with me. She of course burst into tears of joy, and after saying her goodbyes, left everything behind, just as I had, and walked with me to the Shepherd's Garden."

"What about the soccer team?"

"The *football* club," my father corrected, as I rolled my eyes with a smile, "was left to Tommy. And though he hated to see his sister go, he adored her all the more for endowing him with such a treasure."

"So then what happened with you and M- you and Cassia?"

"Great, great things," he said, "but I'll get to that later." And then my father leaned in with another glance over his shoulder. "Now comes the scary part."

"What?"

"The danger your uncle and I were to face-"

"What danger?"

"The Dragon..."

Chapter Eleven

So everything was coming together nicely; Drostan and Crystal were in love, Cassia and I were in love, and we were all staying in the Shepherd's Garden. Cassia and I had planted our seeds side by side, just like Drostan and Crystal, and our two plants were growing straight away, but I'll get to that later.

Every moment it seemed, we learned more and more from the Shepherd about his interesting ways, and somehow it brought the five of us closer all the time. It was like we were all one happy family.

But one day, after having spent several weeks together with the Shepherd, the peace of the garden was interrupted. Tommy rushed into the meadow as we were enjoying an afternoon picnic.

"Something terrible has happened in the Kingdom!" he panted. Seeing his torn clothes, stained with the blood from his visible cuts, I assumed he'd taken a beating from the Diggers and Tree Sprites. Panting as he was, he must have run nearly the whole way.

"Tommy!" Cassia jumped up, which caused me to jump up, which caused Drostan to jump up, which caused Crystal to stand as well.

"What's happened?" I asked, my voice expressing the near panic we all felt.

"Da's gone..." Tommy panted, confused tears making trails through the soot and dried blood on his face.

"What do you mean?!" asked Cassia in a full-out panic, and I saw her hands begin to shake.

"The f- the flames were," Tommy stuttered between gasping pants, "were everywhere... I think he's..."

"Da?" Cassia collapsed into me, and I held her in my arms as she shook with sobs.

"A few days ago, after a game," Tommy began, trying to calm himself enough to explain, "I saw the shepherd coming across the field."

Drostan, Crystal, and I turned to look at the Shepherd, who had joined us for the picnic and was still sitting on the picnic blanket.

"No," Tommy said, "the *other* shepherd."

"The Wolf," said the Shepherd, taking another sip of the drink he held.

"*The Wolf*," said Drostan and I, glancing to each other with recognition.

"He came across the field to me," Tommy continued, paying little notice, "walked right up to me. 'All this came from one little seed?' he asked me. 'Well the uniforms came from Thomas and Penny's shop,' I said to him."

Tommy took another grief-stricken gasp before continuing, "'Hamish crafted the goals and whatnot,' I said to him, 'and the field was painted by one of Gunty's mates. But aye, overall, the club started by one little leather leaf seed.' 'Well then,' he said, 'looks as though you've put your seed to good use.' 'I can't take the credit,' I said to him, 'it was Branan and Cassia built this place up from the ground.' Just trying to give credit where it belonged is all."

"Aye, and right good of you, Tommy," I said, not knowing what else to say.

"But it isn't good," Tommy interrupted. "That's what I'm trying to tell you. After I told him about the seed being yours, the shep- er, the Wolf, he asked me about *my* seed."

"And what did you tell him?" asked the Shepherd, suddenly so serious that we all turned to look at him.

Tommy paused with a somewhat guilty look, then swallowed hard, "I told him the truth."

"Which is what?" asked the Shepherd.

"That I haven't touched it. I don't even remember where it is. For the longest time, I tended the plow shop with Da, and then I was given the football club. Going from my father's seed to Branan's, I never paid a mind to my own."

"This is a problem," said the Shepherd.

The five of us looked at each other, bewildered by the Shepherd's gravity. We understood something was terrible wrong, but weren't quite sure what. Drostan asked the obvious question, "*What's* a problem, Sir?"

"The Wolf came to you," began the Shepherd, looking back to Tommy, "because he knows well his rights."

"His rights?" I asked.

"As my adversary," the Shepherd clarified. "He's long coveted my kingdom. My kingdom is built upon the growing of seeds, the seeds I give as gifts to my sheep. Any unplanted seed that goes sour gives the Wolf and his beast rights to the wasteful sheep's livelihood."

"His beast?" asked Drostan in a tone that suggested he wasn't sure he really wanted the answer.

"Aye," Tommy answered the Shepherd, wide-eyed, "that's what I've come to tell you. The Dragon has inhabited the field, my father's home, and all the land near the football club. He's made it his lair. "

Drostan and I along with the girls let out a simultaneous gasp.

"The green of that land is gone," Tommy continued in a somber tone. "The ground is blackened with the soot of the Dragon's flames. His ash expands out into the Kingdom further by the hour. His thick, black smoke blots out the sky. He has walled his lair with boulders from the clefts of the Distant Mountains and has surrounded his walls with a black moat. Anyone who approaches is spat upon with the flames of his smoking nostrils." Here his voice broke at the thought of the land he loved so much having been made so destitute. Cassia wrapped her arms around him in best efforts to comfort him.

"What can be done?" I asked.

"It's my fault," said Tommy, falling to his knees in remorseful tears, "Da is gone and a dragon lives in the Kingdom." Cassia tried to pat his head, but was unsure exactly what to do with grief as strong as her brother's.

The Shepherd graciously reached his arms out to Tommy, "My son, such things have happened in times past. All is not lost." Tommy looked up and then, slowly standing again, went into the Shepherd's open arms. The comfort that he couldn't quite get from Cassia, though she loved him, he found in the Shepherd's arms.

Suddenly Crystal perked up, wide-eyed with inspiration, her fist raised in front of her, "What we need is a bloody fighter-" realizing her brash tone, she looked embarrassedly to the Shepherd, "excuse me." And then she amended a bit more softly, "What we-what we need is a fighter."

"Aye," said the Shepherd, releasing Tommy with one final pat to his back, "a warrior to take up arms, face the Dragon, and take back what has been stolen from the Kingdom." His tone immediately impassioned my brother and I, so that we felt we could take not only this dragon but seven more.

"What about *two* warriors?" asked Drostan, glancing to me with that same look in his eye that he always got when the Rangers played Man U.

"Two warriors," repeated the Shepherd, rubbing his chin. "That's not so bad a plan."

So Drostan and I mentally prepared ourselves, at least, the best we could, to go face the Dragon. Of course, we had no idea what that really meant, understand.

Aside from the one experience with Hawk, we'd only ever heard of dragons in fairy tales and the like.

The Shepherd said that we would need a special kind of sword to even have any effect at all. With a regular sword, he said, even the strongest sword that man could forge, we'd not stand a chance but for it to melt or break in the midst of battle against such a beast as this. He said he'd have to craft us each one himself. So he called for the fairies of the meadow.

After a few moments we heard a sort of buzz, like distant chatter, followed by the huge swarm of fairies coming into the meadow. There were so many of them. Dros and I had seen them before in the front meadow of course, but never all together at once. I hadn't realized there were so many.

Being as small as they were, one could be anywhere at any given time and no one would be the wiser. I wondered then, being as there were so many, if there had been one near me at all times since I'd entered the Kingdom. The thought was somewhat of a comfort, being as they worked for the Shepherd.

The five of us moved out of the way as the fairies encircled the Shepherd.

There was an awed hush among the fairies, and it was sensed that these beautiful little beings held a corporate audience with the Shepherd to be an honor of high importance.

"Where is Faith?" asked the Shepherd solemnly, searching out over the fluttering crowd surrounding him.

"Here," came a voice from the group, and the beautiful, little fairy fluttered in from the encircling multitude to the Shepherd, as her peers looked after her in honor that she would be called out individually.

She lowered her head, in gracious humility, offering something of a floating bow. "At your service, my lord," she said in her soft, pretty voice.

"Thank you, my sweet lass," he said, tipping his head to her, "for a service is precisely what I need of you. Do you know the flower *Ergon*?"

"Yes, my lord," she answered eagerly. "There is a large bed of Ergon on the shadow side of Spring Mountain."

"Very well," he said with a nod. "Go and retrieve two of them to bring back to me."

"Yes, my lord."

Faith fluttered off in the direction of the mountains and I noticed for the first time that she was a bit smaller than most of her sisters. She couldn't have been very strong. And her eyes were soft, sweet, innocent; she didn't appear any wiser or more cunning than any of the others. I wondered if the Shepherd had chosen her specifically for a reason, or just picked a name at random.

Tommy leaned in closer to me to speak privately. "What's going to happen?" he asked, wiping his eyes. "Will you and Dros save the Kingdom?" He looked expectantly, hopefully at each of us. I realized he was placing great faith in us.

"Tommy," I interrupted, "I'm sorry about your da. I've nothing to say. I- I don't know what will happen, but I swear to do whatever I can. Dros and I will stop at nothing to make things right."

As the moments passed, and we waited for Faith's return with the flowers, I held Cassia close, consoling her as she cried, and when Faith returned with the Ergon, Cassia was able to stand on her own.

"Faith, come stand beside me," commanded the Shepherd, as the rest of the assembly quieted to silence. Faith placed the two flowers prostate at the foot of the Shepherd, then fluttered to hover at his side.

A deafening stillness had settled in all the meadow as the Shepherd stood before everyone. Then he whispered to the Ergon one single word, "Courage." And that was it.

As if nothing else needed to be done, the Shepherd handed each of us our flower saying, "Your weapons."

How stupid was this? Out of respect for the Shepherd, I was careful not to show it on my face, but I'm sure my expression must have betrayed this ridiculous situation. I took the flower all the same; what else was I to do? And strangely enough, Drostan said not a word, nor showed any trace of this absurdity on his face, almost as if he understood something I didn't.

"Now take up arms, my brave warriors," the Shepherd finally continued, "and win back that which was stolen."

Chapter Twelve

"Are you nervous?" I asked Drostan.

We had been making our way down Spring Mountain as quickly as the slope would allow. After four hours, we were now about another hour from the mountain's base, or so we assumed. We weren't entirely sure due to the fog that had settled around us over an hour ago.

"That we won't be able to defeat the Dragon and win back the Kingdom and all that?"

"Aye."

"Of course I've thought about it, but for the moment, I suppose I'm more concerned with lunch."

I deadpanned, surprised by his nonchalance.

"Seriously," he raised his brow, "you know I'm not much a fan of barbeque, and if everything's as charred as Tommy says, then-"

"You don't seem to be taking this very seriously," I interrupted, slightly irritated by his attitude.

"I realize the importance of it all," he answered after a moment, "but there's no sense in worrying. I know the Shepherd; he'd never send us off to our deaths."

"Aye, but maybe you could have just a bit more respect for loss..."

My brother's face turned red with embarrassment. "I'm sorry," he said contritely. "I didn't mean to- you're right, I'm sorry. You were very close to Jack; I didn't mean to be insensitive."

I didn't really want to think about everything so soon after his death, so I just continued to move forward, seeing that we were coming upon the mountain forests, and walked in silence. I had no intention of punishing my brother with silence, understand, I just didn't know what I felt, and I wasn't really ready to decide what that was.

We traveled through the forest for what seemed like forever, before I realized it was getting very cold. I pulled my jacket a bit more snugly around my shoulders, though it wasn't quite thick enough against the frigid air. I rubbed my arms with my hands. Suddenly my stomach rumbled, reminding me that I was as hungry as I was cold.

"Do you want to stop for a bite?"

"Aye, that's it," answered Drostan in agreement, rubbing his hands together. "What've we got?"

"I've got a bit of bread in my pack."

"Bread?" he asked incredulously. "What're we, Sam and Frodo? Couldn't you've brought some actual food? We each know a baker, a chef-"

"What about you?" I asked in accusation, deciding to interrupt. When Drostan got going, he could keep it up for longer than most people would think. "Didn't you save back some chicken from the picnic?"

"Aye, I nearly forgot!" he beamed, as he reached into his pack. "I've got some, let's see," he said as he dug, "some chicken, a bit of bacon, a biscuit, er-" he rummaged further through his pack, "scratch that, *two* biscuits…"

Knowing now that we had a makeshift feast, we made a small fire, sat to eat, and enjoyed what little we could amidst so serious a journey. Once we'd finished and put out the fire, Drostan confirmed what I'd already been thinking, "Has it gotten colder?"

"Seems to have," I replied, again trying to use my hands to warm my arms.

Then I saw his eyes focus on something in the distance, and he pointed as he drew his body a little taller, "That's a snow drift!"

"What!?" I turned to look.

He groaned, "We must've crossed over onto Winter Mountain!"

"Have we taken a wrong turn?"

"Must've."

I stated what we were both thinking; "Now we won't be able to make the Kingdom by nightfall."

"Aye. And we can't spend the night out here. What if the Tree Sprites come? We should find some shelter." He began looking around.

"Aye," I agreed, just before noticing a shadow on the snow just under a mile away. "What about that cave?" I asked, pointing.

He looked the direction I was pointing, "Good a place as any, I suppose," he said. So we made our way into the snow and onto

Winter Mountain.

The cave appeared by all accounts from the outside to be a mere den, but this appearance was deceitful. Once inside, we saw that it delved far, far back, deep and dark into the earth. The unknown enormity of it was now, I must admit, somewhat unsettling.

Its icy crags were an obvious blend of rock and ice, frozen and refrozen over decades or centuries. Though the stalactites and stalagmites stood everywhere, like pillars of diversity, the rock of this cave was united in permanence. It was like one huge hollowed out rock, solid to the very last, a prison. I was glad we had set up our makeshift camp so near the opening.

As the sky's light had already begun to dim, we started a fire; just big enough for heat and light, but small enough to keep from attracting any attention to ourselves. Drostan sat nearly atop it to thaw out his frosty bum, while I tried to arrange my pack into a sort of makeshift pillow.

That was when we heard the rumbling. It sounded frighteningly like the growl of some enormous beast.

"What was that?" I startled, jumping to my feet and looking back into the dark catacombs behind us.

"I've no idea," answered Drostan, focusing his eyes back into the dark as well, "but it certainly wasn't a very happy sound."

"Agreed," I confirmed, picturing the monsters from any given horror film.

We stood for a moment, our ears straining.

"We should check it out, I think," Drostan finally said.

"Not sure I like that idea," I said warily, "going in weaponless."

Dros gave me a look I couldn't quite define. "What about our swords?" he said, holding out the Ergon flower.

I looked at him incredulously. He obviously had to have been joking, which was par for him, joking at a time like this, but he looked so serious. "Tally's in," I finally said, "you're entirely off it."

"What do you mean?"

Slightly irritated, I humored him, "That's a bloody flower, mate."

There was just the hint of a grin to his face as he spoke, "Didn't the Shepherd say these were our weapons?"

"Aye, but-"

"And," he interrupted, "has he ever given you reason to distrust him?"

I pondered that for a moment and realized that my brother had a point. Almost at that very moment, I realized he *wasn't* holding a flower but a brilliant broadsword. Somewhat aghast, I dropped my hands to my sides. Hearing a shing, I followed the sound to find a sword identical to Drostan's hanging at my own side.

It took me a few moments to process it all, and my brother seemed to understand somehow, giving me space and silence.

After enough time had passed, he spoke, "With sword in hand, I see no reason not to find the source of these bothersome sounds."

"All the same," I disagreed without much thought, still picturing monsters from the films, "I don't think it's the best of ideas."

"Well *I'm* not just going to lie here all night and wonder what might come out of the pit and eat me," he said, getting up and starting toward the sound. And after a moment's thought, I acknowledged that this was a valid concern and agreed to follow him with a torch, and we went deeper into the cave.

As we crept along in the dark, with only the glow of the one small torch, we heard more grumblings, getting louder as we went.

"Sounds like we're getting closer," whispered my brother.

"Aye. What do you suppose it is?"

"Probably an angry giant who smells the blood of an Englishman."

Even in a situation like this, he was incorrigible. "Is it not possible for you to be serious? Like, are you defective? Are you just not able?"

"Maybe," he answered with a deadpan. "I'd never really thought about it. It would certainly explain a lot..."

"Keep going." I nudged him forward, ignoring the annoyance he presented me. It was then that we saw it.

Around the next bend, a standing collection of icy pillars, light from the torch showed a reflection off the ice of the cave wall and we saw in the reflection a huge beast of some kind. He appeared to be sleeping, lying in a heap on the ice floor, snoring. His furry mound of a body swelled slightly out and back in with the rhythm of sleep. Not very vividly, as it were, from the poor reflection, I could barely make out whitish fur, stained with what must've been years of savagery, huge padded feet, talon-shod hands, and some sort of tusk-like horns atop his head.

At the sight of such a hideous beast, my brother and I both startled, terrified, and I accidentally dropped the torch with a loud thud and fiery-light refractions that shot in every direction. The beast growled loudly, wakened from his slumber. He jumped to his massive, hairy feet, standing tall and ferocious.

"Run!" I yelled, and we both turned and started back around the icy pillars.

The Snow Beast roared in fury as he came after us. I heard a crunching, crashing sound as he ripped two huge armfuls of rock and ice from the cave wall.

The huge, chaotic bundle of rock and ice came whirring through the air over our heads and crashed to the ground twenty feet or so ahead of us, blocking off our escape and trapping us in with the beast. We came to a screeching halt.

Terrified, I forced myself to turn and face him.

"Stop it," I said in the calmest, firmest tone I could manage under the circumstances. I wasn't sure why I did it. Honestly, it was the only thing I could think of at the time, but somehow it just felt right.

The Snow Beast stopped dead in his tracks and cocked his head to look at me with a confused expression. I could see in his big, blank eyes that his tiny pea brain could not process the current situation.

Drostan turned, still shaking with fear beside me, and looked at me disconcertedly.

"What are you doing!?" his voice strained.

"Just be still," I whispered back, "I've an idea."

"Hope it's a bloody good one."

Slowly, cautiously, but still with the stern, corrective look in my eye, I pointed up to him. "There's no need for you to be so angry," I said. "My brother and I just wanted a safe place to sleep for the night, so we stopped off in your cave. I'm sorry we woke you, but roaring and crashing about won't put you back to sleep."

The Snow Beast focused on my eyes, and I had no reason to believe he understood a single word I said. Still, slowly dropping my hand back to my side, I continued. "That's what you want, isn't it? You just want to go back to peaceful sleep. Well, my brother and I can help you with that."

Then, with fear that I refused to show, I slowly reached up and patted his furry arm. I motioned for Drostan to mirror me as I cautiously walked around to the side of the Snow Beast, softly rubbing the fur of his back, or at least, what I could reach. Even though the beast still looked a bit confused, I saw his eyes begin to dim a little.

"Aye, there you are, wee beastie," I crooned, "lie down and rest your wee, weary eyes."

He rumbled quietly, lying down as we accommodated his comfort.

"We should sing to him," whispered Drostan, "sing him to sleep, like Ma used to."

"Good idea. *Flower of Scotland?*"

"Ma always sang *Jesus Loves Me.*"

And so we sang, Drostan taking the harmony; and by the time the Bible had told him so, the Snow Beast was sound asleep. After which, we decided it was safe, and went back to our campfire to sleep.

That night, I suppose due to the events of the evening and the freezing temperatures, I dreamed the strangest dream.

I was with the Snow Beast and we were having a conversation. No growling, no slamming his fists or raking his big horns along the ice, he was calmly, sensibly talking with me about his frustrations.

"So, why are you always so cranky, Sir?" I asked the Snow Beast.

"Because I just want to sleep," he told me, "and the Shepherd keeps coming in and waking me up."

"Well, I know the Shepherd personally, and he's a good man; he wouldn't do something just to be mean. I'm sure there's a reason."

"But why can't everyone just leave me alone? I'm fine in this cave by myself. I don't bother anybody. I don't go out in the Kingdom and hurt anyone or change anything. I just want to keep to myself, be as I've always been, and sleep in peace."

"You say you want peace, Sir, but why then did you become so violent when my brother and I just happened upon you? You tried to trap us in."

156

"Aye, I'm sorry about that. I never set out to be mean; it's just my first reaction. Usually, anyone who comes in here wants to get me outside of my cave or change something about the way I live. The only thing I know to do is to trap them in here with me."

"Do you attack the Shepherd when he comes in to wake you?"

"Of course not; he's the Shepherd."

"-I guess it would be difficult for *anyone* not to love the Shepherd."

"Well, aye I suppose; I've never thought about it that way. It's just that, well, you *have* to love the Shepherd. It's the rules."

Chapter Thirteen

Waking up the following morning next to a pile of frozen coals, I didn't put much thought into the dream I'd had; I was just glad to be leaving Winter Mountain. My brother and I trekked off in the direction we'd come the previous day, back across Summer Mountain, and as we traveled, I resolved aloud, "This whole thing will be set right before the sun leaves the sky tonight."

My brother didn't say anything for a moment. "You sure of that?" he finally said.

"I'm deciding it as we speak," I said with a slight smile, though I meant every word.

"About how long do you think it'll take to get to the forests at the base of Spring Mountain?"

"I've no idea," I answered. "But I plan to make it to the Kingdom well before nightfall." And so we traveled, frustrated that we were backtracking, and impatient at the slowness of our progression.

Across nearly the whole of Summer Mountain, there was little sound between us save our footfalls, as neither of us saw a need for words. As I listened to the rhythm of it, I was reminded of the similar rhythm of Cassia's feet and mine as we'd dribbled a football, passing it between us along the waterside. So many hours we'd spent together by the loch with a football or without, just to be together.

"I shouldn't have left her," I said, jolting out of my reverie.

"Cassia?" Drostan asked.

"Aye. Of all times, I shouldn't have run off so soon after-"

Drostan interrupted, "Nothing different could be done. Something *needed* to be done, brother."

I knew he was right, but I still felt guilty. "How'd you suppose they're doing, Cassia and Tommy?"

"As good as can be expected, I'm sure, considering. They'll be fine though; they need to grieve for a bit; it's natural."

"I just hate to feel helpless. It's like-" I trailed off.

"When Ma died?" Drostan finished, knowing exactly what I meant.

"Exactly. We wanted to be with Da, but nothing we said or did made any difference."

"We don't know that."

"It sure seemed that way," I countered.

"Aye, but that's just it;" he said, "it *seemed* that way. We don't know but that it might have meant the world to him. That his two teenage sons would give every moment of six months to tend the farm with him, just to be by his side through all that."

I pondered that for a silent moment.

"A valid point, I suppose," I conceded, before grinning to him, "truly you are a scholar, Sir." I gave a mock bow.

"Indeed, they call me Robert Burns."

"Hm," I smiled, "because of all that Haggis, I suppose?"

"Good meal, that," he grinned, "but I'll skip to the dram straightaway, if it suits you."

"Ha," I laughed. "Footballers; you're all the same."

Another hour or so of walking along brought us finally to the forest at the base of Spring Mountain. I took in the scent of fresh pine and spruce and my mind flashed with scenes of the farm.

"Smells like home," I smiled.

"The farm, you mean?"

"Aye." I breathed deep again as if to punctuate the feeling.

"Indeed... D'you miss it sometimes?"

"I think of it now and again, but I can't seem to leave the Shepherd. I feel a sort of belonging to him, as strange as it seems-"

"No," he interrupted, "I totally know what you mean; it's a sort of conundrum."

"Did you just say 'conundrum'?"

He grinned, "Think I might've-"

Just then, I felt a little flick on the back of my neck. I brushed at my neck, then shivered at feeling something scamper along and clench painfully to my shoulder.

"Owe!" I said just below a shout, as I thrust a reflexive swat aimlessly into the air near my shoulder.

"Is that what I think it is?" asked Drostan, and I was alarmed at the look on his face.

I turned my face to look, and saw what looked like something between a fairy and a dragonfly. Its little face was very bug-like, and yet I could still see hints of the fairy it once was. It watched my eyes with absolute hate and fury.

Without warning, it released its little itchy spines from my shoulder and rushed off, jetting through the air with a zipping sound.

Drostan and I looked at each other wide-eyed, knowing, fearing what was to come. And it came shortly after: a low angry buzzing sound. The buzzing grew louder every second the sprites drew nearer.

"It sounds like there's a lot," said Drostan, still wide-eyed with fear.

As the sprites filtered through the trees toward us, I saw there were far too many to count. Though there surely couldn't be nearly as many as the fairies of the meadow, there were still indeed many.

"Probably at least a hundred per each of us?" I asked in short breaths.

"At the very least."

"What do we do?"

"Hawk!" he suddenly remembered.

We waited, watching the skies hopefully.

Nothing...

There appeared to be no rescue this time, no massive, flapping wings. No screeching, echoing caw. No sound at all, save the pounding in my ears of my speeding heart, and the zipping sound of the swarming sprites that furiously surrounded us.

"Hawk!" we both yelled this time, more desperately. Still

nothing.

One sprite came out from the chaotic swarm, approached us, and demanded in a scratchy voice, "Who are you!? And by what right have you entered the Forest of Phobos!?"

I spoke in the most authoritative voice I could muster, "We have come from the Shepherd's Garden, sent by the Shepherd as warriors."

"Warriors, ha!" he barked disdainfully. "You haven't even drawn your swords."

Remembering the sword, I started to reach for its hilt, but couldn't move my hand. I looked down to my wrists to see that they were tied together by some sort of vine. My eyes shot over to Drostan's wrists to see that he was in the same predicament.

"What's this?" I thought aloud, confusedly.

"Shut your mouth, sheep!" the little sprite screamed in fury.

"How are we going to get out of this?" whispered my brother, and I noticed that another knotted vine was now binding each of our forearms.

"Just do whatever they say," I whispered back, before feeling another vine binding my ankles. The chaotic swarm then joined what I assumed to be their little general of sorts, and they all surrounded us.

Now that we were both bound at the ankles, it took very little for the wall of sprites to topple us over. I braced myself for the impact of my back and head against the ground, but was surprised to find that Drostan and I had been pushed over by the wall of sprites in front of us to land on the hovering wall of sprites behind us, who promptly lifted us into the air.

Now hovering a few feet above the forest floor, we were carried deeper into the forest. I heard the low rumbling of the sprites, the chanting in some ancient tongue, and the rhythm of it reminded me of some sort of ancient Wiccan ritual.

We were woven through the trees, this way and that, turn after turn, for what seemed like hours, all the while stopping every half hour or so. When we would stop, we would be stood upright, our feet set on the ground, and we would be furiously screamed at by the little general. It all reminded me slightly of what I'd read of Auschwitz and Nazi Germany.

Every so often, Drostan or I would notice another knotted vine binding us in a new place, the forearms, the legs, the shoulders, the ankles. The vines were tied, though no one came and tied them there; it was like some dark magic. It seemed to be timed to precision, like there was some sort of reason or pattern to the acquisition of new bonds, but I couldn't nail it down in my mind.

When we would stop, the little sprite general would have us stood to our feet and then zip back and forth in front of us, screaming.

He would insult us, demand immediate answers of us, and stab us, prodding us with his little itchy, bristly spines. He would rile up the swarm around him, accusing us of one thing immediately after accusing us of just the opposite. None of it made any sense.

"Who are you!?" he would demand.

"We already told you! We're-"

"Have you come to the Forest of Phobos as the Shepherd's spies? Answer!"

"No, I- we just-"

"To whom is your allegiance!?"

"We told you, we're with the Shep-"

"If you are with the Shepherd, then why have you left his garden?! High treason!" he turned and screamed to his legion. The chaotic swarm roared, "Traitors!"

"What? I thought you were-"

"Silence!"

Then after several minutes of this, we would be hoisted up once again and carried through the forest. It was just about the same every time, except that we were bleeding more after each stop, and after hours and hours of the being carried, stopping, being screamed at, and being once again hoisted up and carried, Drostan whispered an observation to me.

"We're going in circles." He motioned with his eyes up to a treetop, "I've seen that same owl probably six times in the past couple of hours."

My eyes followed his up to the owl, at which time I noticed it had gotten dark.

"We've wasted a whole day going in bloody circles?"

"I'm afraid," Drostan embarrassedly admitted. "I know they're very little creatures, but the magic of these tree sprites frightens me."

"I'm in the same lot with you, mate," I conceded. "Should we try calling Hawk again?"

"But what if he doesn't come? It'll just make them angry."

"Hawks have excellent hearing, don't they? ...*Hawk*," I whispered.

He rolled his eyes, "It's '*eyes like a hawk*,' dufus, not ears."

All the same, a deafening screech echoed through the sky, and I heard enormous wings flapping somewhere in the distance. The sound had a curious effect on me. Whereas moments earlier I was despairing and afraid, now suddenly I was filled with hope and courage once again. Seeing this fulfillment of my deep hope was empowering, and at that moment the vines dissipated. Whether they dissolved to nothing or simply fell off us, I've no way of knowing, but my brother and I were free of our bonds.

"What the?" Drostan looked over to me in surprise.

The atmosphere around us, everything down to the scent of the air, seemed to change as Hawk swooped in with talons bared, piercing caws echoing off the trees. Our feet hit the ground with a low thud, and we heard the tree sprites scatter.

"Back to the trees!" screamed the terrified little general, and I saw all of the hundreds of sprites scatter and bury themselves in their little tree nooks.

As the leaves and whatnot settled, Hawk perched on a large branch, looking down at us with what must have been a smile, at least for a hawk.

"That was easy enough," mumbled Drostan.

"Thank you again, Sir," I said with a nod.

"Did you not hear us earlier?" added Drostan, and though I feared he shouldn't be so blunt, I wondered the same.

"I cannot apologize. I rescue in the manner that I rescue. It may not always seem to make sense, but it's always for the best. I don't make mistakes. But," he continued, "I told you I would help you, and I haven't let you down yet. You were wrong not to trust me."

"...Understood," we said simultaneously, after an ashamed glance to one another.

With this, Hawk remounted the sky and soared away with a deafening caw. We watched as he disappeared somewhere amidst the horizon, and then it set in, "We're spending the night in the forest."

"Looks like," I breathed, frustrated.

"D'you think we'll have any more trouble with the tree sprites?"

"Don't think so; they seemed quite scared of Hawk."

So we built a small fire and bed down for the night. My dream this night was equally strange as the night before. I dreamed that I was conversing with one of the trees. "Those vines... How did they- they seemed to appear from nothing to bind us. What were they?"

The great tree looked down to me with his wise, ancient eyes, "The vines are Phobos. That is why the tree sprites call my home the Forest of Phobos, though that is not its rightful name."

"The sprites are confusing. Whose side are they on anyway?"

"They are on the side of no one. Self-consumed little beasts; their one, single aim is to be against the Shepherd. Their allegiance seems to shift because confusion is their ally. The more confusion they cause their victims, the more Phobos their victims grow."

"Wait- what?"

"Phobos comes from within."

The next thing I knew, I'd waken up to the daylight filtering in through the trees.

Chapter Fourteen

Once breakfast had been sufficiently procured and consumed, and the coals of our campfire were safely cold, we set off for the Drylands. The cold camp we left was apparently further down the mountain than we'd thought, for it was only maybe half an hour through the forests before we noticed the trees beginning to thin.

"Looks like we're coming up on the Drylands."

"Aye," I agreed.

"What do you think about the Diggers?"

"What do you mean?" I asked.

"I mean, are you worried at all?" he clarified.

I thought a second. "A bit."

"Have we got a plan?"

"Not really, let's think. What do we know about them?"

"Well," he paused, "they're greedy."

"Aye, and -wait, what?" -Greedy didn't make sense to me.

"The Shepherd said they want inside our heads."

"Aye, that he did...?" I let it hang as a question. Of course I remembered the Shepherd saying that, but I didn't see the connection.

"Well, they've got their own heads, I assume. What need have they in ours?"

"I think you might be looking at this from a different angle than what was-"

Just then, out of the dry, cracked, sandy earth, I saw a mound begin to form several feet ahead of us. Out of this shifting mound of dust, I saw a pointy, wet snout poke up, sniff the air, and then quickly submerge again.

"Hey," said Drostan to me in a surprised, confused tone, "that's Old Man Campbell!"

"What?" I looked in the direction he pointed and sure enough, Old Man Campbell stood shaking his wrinkly old fist, just like I remembered him.

"Drostan Williams! You keep out of my orchard!"

"What are you talking about, Sir?" Drostan tried to hide a snicker. "I haven't stolen a single, solitary apple from your yard since I was seven years old..."

"I've seen you in there, you little bugger! Get out of my yard!"

"So what do I do?" he turned to me laughing, "I know this isn't real; Old Man Campbell's been dead for years. It's got to be the Diggers. How do I make it go away?"

"How should I know?"

Just then, something came zipping through the air.

"Owe, shite!" yelled Drostan, as a sharp rock glanced off his arm. "You old bugger, that bloody hurt!"

"You heard the man," I laughed. "Get out of his yard."

The old man whipped another stone at Drostan, this one catching him right in the face.

"This is starting to get a bit serious," I said, no longer laughing. I was honestly afraid my brother might lose an eye or something if this nonsense kept up. "Alright you," I yelled at the old man. "We know what you are, Digger! Now bury yourself back in your hole!"

With this, Mr. Campbell disappeared and a little scale-armored, rodent-like creature scampered off and buried himself in the earth. I turned to see Drostan rubbing a big, red bump on his cheek.

"How's your face, pal?" I grinned.

He looked at me irritated, "Aye, sure it's easier to laugh when you're not the one received the wallop."

We walked on.

It wasn't but a few steps forward that I saw another wet nose poke up from the dirt and disappear back down into the same. Once the mound of dirt had stilled, I heard Drostan whisper reverently, "Ma?"

I turned to see him looking off into the distance, and then followed his eyes to see what it was that had acquired his attention. It was Ma.

I couldn't believe it. She looked just the same as she had the night before she died; beautiful, smiling the way she used to. She'd always had the most heart-warming smile, folks used to say, with eyes that lit up a room.

Scenes from that night years ago flashed liked slides through my head. Ma had made Wellington Squares with peanut butter, your uncle Drostan's favorite, and we sat near the fireplace to enjoy it with the dusk. Da made a joke about taking out his pipes and playing in a room so small just to ruin the evening, and Ma, with a wink, thanked him kindly not to.

I remembered, the next morning, going out with Da, in a worried search for her; she'd gone off somewhere, walking in her sleep again. I remembered seeing her body, cold and lifeless, as Mr. McMillan and Doc Willis pulled her up from the well.

I felt two tears slide down my face and splash to the dust between my feet as I walked across the cracked, thirsty earth of the Drylands toward Ma. She reached her arms out to me with a smile.

"Ah, Branan," she said, "how I've missed you."

"I've missed you as well, Ma," I whispered between tears.

"You've been through enough, haven't you lad?" she whispered, brushing the tear from my cheek.

"What do you mean?"

"I mean, you lost me, your Da's at home dying in his bed, your friend Jack has died; haven't you suffered enough? And all the while, your sweet Cassia awaits your return."

"Well, aye, but-"

"Take your brother, will you, and go back to the garden. Both of you go back to your women. Don't go off searching for vain honor hunting a dragon."

"It's not for vanity's sake, Ma, I swear it." But even as I said it, I wasn't sure. It did seem extremely prideful for me to be off on some quest while Cassia, my sweet Cassia, was back at the garden hurting and in need of me.

"All the same, lad, turn around-"

"Don't listen to her, Branan," Drostan interrupted. "That's not really Ma."

"What are you on about? I can see her right there," I pointed. "Are you blind?"

"It's not really Ma, Branan," he said again. "It's the Diggers; they're in your head."

"What?"

"You've got to block them out. Tell them what they are."

"What?" I was so confused. "How? What's this mean?" I turned again to her, still crying, "Ma, is it- Are you not- Is it you?"

"Turn back, son," she said again, smiling sadly. "This dragon is not your responsibility. You've suffered enough already."

"Branan!" my brother yelled this time. "Look at me, brother! You've got to think! You have to remember, Ma's gone! She's not really here! It's not real!"

Again, I saw in my mind my ma's lifeless body, being pulled from the well. Drostan and I were sixteen then; I could remember it with perfect clarity. I remembered the wake, seeing her lying there; I remember dealing with the loss, accepting what could not be changed.

"No," I said with a sniff. "You're just the Diggers. Bury yourselves." And once Ma had disappeared, they did just as I'd told them to.

Drostan looked to me. "Are you..."

"I'm alright," I said, turning to my brother, wiping my eyes. "Let's go."

Drostan looked at me for a moment to be sure.

"I promise," I assured him, "I'm ready. Let's keep moving."

...After about an hour of walking over a sea of absolute drought, my head became a bit dizzy, and I looked down into my pack to see if I had any water left. Finding the one bottle that remained, I sat down for a moment on a sort of rocky mound as Drostan did the same.

"You first," he said as I offered him the bottle. I thanked him and uncapped it, lifting the not-so-refreshing, lukewarm water to my mouth.

After we'd passed the bottle for a couple turns each, we sat for a moment to rest. It was only seconds after seeing another pointed, wet snout poke up from the ground that I heard Drostan speaking under his breath in an incredulous tone.

"What's he doing here?"

"Dros?" I asked.

"Cam?" he called out. "Hey, Cam! We've got water over here if you're thirsty, mate."

I looked up in the direction Drostan was calling, and saw none other than Cameron Ferguson, one of our mates from Golspie. I hadn't seen him in years. We all used to play football on the same team when we were teenagers, up until his injury. I could see he still had the limp.

He'd broken his ankle one game sliding in for a tackle, and at just the wrong angle apparently. It never really healed back right, so he was left with a limp. Sadly, he could never really play again, at least not with the skill he had before. It made me sad to see that he was still limping.

Then it hit me with obvious clarity: Cam wasn't really there.

"Block it out, Dros. That's not Cam."

But he ignored me. I reached up to his arm, about to grab it with a shake, but thought better of it. Knowing the whole story behind Drostan and Cam, I decided to be silent and let him work it out on his own, at least for the moment. He lifted the bottle up as Cam came closer, "Drink, mate," he said. "Help yourself."

"Oh, so now we're mates and all that?" asked Cam with a smirk, as he retrieved the bottle from Drostan's hand.

"...Haven't we've always been?"

"That's not how I remember it," said Cam after two big gulps. "I remember you being so in love with football that you had no time for a cripple."

"Cam," pleaded Drostan, "I never meant to-"

"We were going to get a flat in Dundee; start a football team; remember that? But you and Branan went off without me. Couldn't let a cripple get in your way of being a football hero."

"...It w- it wasn't like that, Cameron," said my brother, but his remorse could be felt in the air.

"Wasn't it? So you and Branan *didn't* get a flat in Dundee and start a football team?"

"No... We played rugger."

"And I'm certain that's the point I was making," he answered sarcastically.

"All I'm saying is that I- I made some selfish decisions and I'm sorry I wasn't-"

"That's it, spot on: you're a selfish, self-consumed wanker. As long as you get to be the hero on the field, all the rest is rubbish, aye? And now you're going to run off to take a dragon, are you? Won't that be just bloody brilliant; you getting to be the hero? You don't deserve it. You're *not* a hero. You're a sodding wanker, full stop."

Here, I decided to jump in. "None of it's true, Dros. That's not even Cam. It's the Diggers."

I saw recognition flash in his eyes, and Cameron disappeared, leaving the little armored creature to waddle away and bury himself in the earth.

"...It may not have truly been Cameron," he answered after a moment, with a sad look in his eye, "but everything he said was true."

"You made a mistake. It was years ago, Dros."

"...I was so selfish," he continued in his own remorseful world.

"You're not even the same man you were then. You weren't even a *man* at all, for that matter; you were a stupid kid. We both were. You would never do something like that now-"

"How do you *know* that?"

"Because you regret the selfish choices we made back then. If you didn't, you wouldn't have seen Cam just now. Everything that just happened came from *your* head. That's how the Diggers work..."

After such an experience as that, I thought it fitting to give my brother a few moments to get his wits about him. Once he had, we agreed to continue on.

"What should we expect next, d'you suppose?" he asked after a few minutes of walking.

"No idea, but if McMillan's dairy cattle show up, it was *you* who pushed them over."

"Here's what I think," he began after a laugh, "should another memory return to haunt us, we need to figure out a way to use it to our benefit."

"Good idea, but how?"

"Talk to it."

"What?"

"Speak to it. –Just like we've done already. When we speak to the Diggers, they seem to cower in fear; they're only little rodents after all."

"Well that's working great for stopping the memories altogether, but how do you propose we use them to our benefit?"

"When a memory comes, tell it the truth. Like Old Man Campbell, for example. Remember that time when he was sick for a whole month and we took him caramels?"

"Aye."

"Well, when the Diggers made him yell at me, saying, 'get out of my yard,' I should've just said that I was coming over to bring him caramels."

"Like, use a good memory to cancel out the bad?"

"Exactly."

"Well that sounds like a method we could use, but it doesn't look like we'll need to." I pointed out, less than a hundred yards in front of us, to a gorgeous, green meadow.

"The Back Meadow!" said Drostan happily. "We've made it!"

"Only about a mile to the Kingdom," I added, slightly less enthusiastic. "Don't forget, mate, we still have a dragon ahead of us."

"Branan!" called a familiar voice from where a new mound had formed just before the start of the Back Meadow.

"...Jack?" I answered.

"Crivens," mumbled Drostan, "another one. It's not Jack, Branan," he reminded me, a hint of worry in his voice, "it's just another Digger."

"Don't worry, brother. I've got this."

"Branan!" Jack continued in panting breaths, as black, charred burn scars began appearing all over him. "The Dragon got to me! I've met my fate, lad! Turn around! Go back or you'll meet the same fate yourself!"

"Here goes," I said under my breath to Drostan. Then I raised my voice, "You're not the Jack I remember. The Jack I knew had the courage of twenty men. 'Turn around and run?' Ballocks! I'll stand and fight, just like you would..."

Jack stopped in his tracks, stood upright, and let out a loud laugh.

"Aye, bloody right I would!" he laughed. Then I saw, as his scars, each and every one, turned from charred burns into glimmering, silver armor, vesting him from shoulders to toes.

"Now you listen to me lads," he said with a firm, instructive resolve, and just the hint of a smile. "You go into that kingdom, you take that dragon, you put his head to the ground, and you remove it."

Chapter Fifteen

After the Drylands, the walk through the Back Meadow was quite refreshing. All the same, we were glad to finally reach the outer wall of the Kingdom; this quest couldn't end soon enough.

Once we'd entered through the back gate, we saw that nothing looked all that different from before, at least not within the first mile or so.

"Don't know what all the fuss is about," shrugged Drostan as we inclined the sloping stone avenue, "everything looks the same as when we lef-"

Drostan's words dropped off mid-sentence, as we crested the slope to see the blackened ruins of the Kingdom lying before us like a wasteland. We both stopped and stood, still and silent, overlooking what was once a beautiful, glimmering, bustling city. Encircling the massive, now blackened city was the fringe of it near the outer wall; the only parts that remained as they once were.

"Bloody hell..." said Drostan in a breath.

"Quite literally, I would think."

Just then, a breeze swept up toward us, carrying with it a rank, foul stench of death and rot.

"Uhg," choked Drostan, "place smells like Liverpool."

Appalled by his light-hearted response, it took me a moment to respond.

"Shut up, would you," I said, "this is serious! Neither one of us have ever faced a dragon before."

"Apologies," he said in a low tone, in response to my vigor.

"We need to prepare," I said sternly, pointing to my head to imply the crafting of plans.

"Technically," said Drostan after a moment, "we *have* faced a dragon before; this very one, it would seem."

I took that into consideration...

"What could we gain from our experience with Hawk," I finally said, thinking aloud.

"We know he can fly and spit flames. Nearly burnt Hawk to a crisp."

"Aye. And we know he's too long to turn very quickly. He's only able to move fast in one direction."

"And he seems to have a vulnerable underbelly; that's where Hawk attacked."

"Aye." I stared off as I worked it over in my brain at every angle.

We'd seen the Dragon in action, but only in one setting: flight. This time we'd be coming upon him afoot. We'd hopefully have a slight upper hand by sneaking in and catching him unaware, but his natural recourse would be to immediately spurt his furious flames, to which we'd have no defense.

My brother and I began walking again.

Once we'd passed the charred remains of Delaina's Dress Shop, my brother asked, "Is that what I think it is?" and I looked up to see him pointing to what looked like the gnarled up carcass of a dead plant.

"My Rubber Plant."

"Looks like it's been uprooted."

"Indeed. It's like a dead, dried up husk."

"And there's another one over there."

I looked where he pointed, several feet away, and saw a large, spongy-looking pod-like object. "You're blind, mate. That's not a dead Rubber Plant. It doesn't look dead at all, actually."

"Aye, you're right," he said, squinting his eyes to examine it more closely.

"Actually, it looks a bit like an egg. –Like a big, spongy egg."

We both stared at it silently, slowly coming to the inevitable conclusion. Finally, Drostan said it aloud, "A dragon egg..."

"Aye," I agreed with concern. "We should take a closer look."

And so we approached the big, spongy, oval object warily. There were no necessarily obvious implications that it was an egg other than that it simply looked like one, but we didn't know what to expect, so we were careful all the same.

"Doesn't show any movement," said Drostan once we'd examined it for a moment.

"All the same, I don't trust it. Let's keep moving."

Once we'd walked along for some time without incident, our nerves calmed down a bit. It was no longer expectation of danger at any given turn, but more a taking in of all that had happened. It made me think of Jack, which of course led me back to Cassia. I wondered what she was doing. I looked at Drostan and saw that he too was deep in thought. Suddenly he spoke.

"The Kingdom is really great and all, but I figured I'd just, you know, be here for awhile, like going on holiday or whatever, and then go back to real life."

"So?"

"I'm just saying, now I'm not so sure I want to leave. I really like the Shepherd, and I feel like the life I've found *here*, with Crystal, couldn't be any better or *more real* back home."

"Indeed. Life in the Kingdom is like a whole new way to live..." And I thought about what I'd just said. "But what if we took it back with us?"

"What?"

"This new way to live. I mean, what if we sort of, *showed* this new way to Da? To Michael? To Cameron- to *everyone* we know? What if we went back and changed everything."

Just then, I saw another egg, standing out in the open by itself, just like the first one.

"Dros," I got his attention, nodding toward the egg.

"So that's number two. How many do you suppose there are?"

"Dunno. More importantly, what do you suppose they're producing? *That's* what worries me."

"Indeed."

Once we'd turned and walked several feet away, we heard a

strange squeaking sound, like the twisting of Styrofoam or something. We turned and saw that the top of the egg was open, so we ran back to look inside. It was empty.

"I don't like this," I said fearfully, horror film scenes once again running relentlessly through my head.

"Agreed. Let's get out of here." And we left the area hurriedly.

As we walked on, I came to a random thought I hadn't considered yet: What if the eggs were nothing to worry about? As if to say, what if we were wrong about the Dragon? What if he *wasn't* our enemy? Maybe Tommy had misunderstood what had happened, and my brother and I were acting upon faulty information.

For that matter, what if the *Wolf* wasn't our enemy? We'd thought of him as our enemy simply because the Shepherd had told us he was. We'd only met the Shepherd a day or so before we'd met the Wolf. We didn't know either one of them that much more than the other. I stewed these thoughts, and all they implied, in my head for a few moments.

"How do we know the Shepherd really is who he says he is?" I finally asked.

"What do you mean?"

"I mean, do we really believe he made all of this just by speaking?" I gestured about us to signify the Kingdom. "I can't say that I'm sure of that. It doesn't make any sense."

My brother contemplated for a moment or two before he replied. "His magic is bigger than what we can understand. At least, that's the way I look at it. If- if everything that exists is limited to what *we* have the capacity to understand, then *Everything That Is* must be a pretty small place."

"Valid point that, but how do we *know* it?"

"I suppose we don't. At least, not with the same certainty that we know grass is green and rocks are hard and-"

"So, for all we know, the Shepherd may have purposely sent us off to our deaths on a fool's errand-"

"That's just pure dead stupid. Where is this coming from anyway? Why do you suddenly not trust him?"

"I just think we're risking a lot based on assump-"

"I know Shepherd is who he says he is because I *know* him," he continued, now with resolve. "Can I prove it in a bloody laboratory? Of course not. Same as I can't prove that I loved Ma; but show me a man who will question my love for Ma and I'll show you a brand new broken nose."

"Another valid point, I suppose, but wha-"

"I've spent hours and hours with Shepherd. We've talked face to face, eye to eye, man to man. He is who he says he is-"

"Another one!" I interrupted, pointing to another egg. "How many of these bloody things are there out here?! ...And, as we've been on the subject of what's what; we keep calling these dragon eggs; how do we know they're not Hawk eggs-"

My brother's jaw dropped, "...I hereby deny your speaking privileges-"

"I'm just saying; we know this side of nothing about Hawk.

We've assumed he's in league with the Shepherd, and that they're on *our* side, but we don't *know* that. We don't even know from where he comes or where he goes to-"

"All we know is that he's been a bloody life-saver. At least twice, as a matter of fact."

So engrossed in the opposing sides of our discourse, we unwittingly walked up to the egg just as it opened. Just as had happened before, there was a squeaking sound as the top of the spongy egg seemed to pry itself open.

Inside, we saw a slimy little writhing thing with reaching tentacles; it was quite disgusting actually. Without warning, it puffed up and leapt out of the egg and onto Drostan's arm.

He panicked.

"Ah shite! Get this bloody thing off me!"

Seeing the little slime ball burrowing its tentacles into my brother's arm, I didn't have time to think. I yanked my sword up quickly and awkwardly, as it was still strapped to my belt, and slammed the hilt into my brother's wrist.

"Owe!" Drostan yelled, his wrist sounding as though it must have cracked in half.

The slimy, wriggling creature hit the ground with a light thud, and by this time I'd finally gotten my sword from the sheath. I plunged the end of my magical sword into the earth, dividing the disgusting little creature into halves with it.

Drostan looked to me, wide-eyed, holding his throbbing wrist.

"No need to break me into pieces!"

"Sorry, brother."

"Let's get out of here. Quickly-" he interrupted himself, looking down at the back of my leg. "But first let's get that off you."

"What?" I asked, trying to crane my neck around to see.

"You've got one."

"But there was only one in that egg. We saw it open."

"Must be from the egg that opened earlier."

My brother took the sword from my hand and pried the slimy little thing off; it had burrowed its tentacles in deep by now. As it fell from my leg, I felt something change.

"That's quite strange..." I felt a revived sense of clarity.

"What?"

"All those things I was saying earlier..."

"About Shepherd and Hawk planning evil plots against us?" he asked sarcastically.

"Aye... It's like, somehow, it... it seems foolish to me now."

"Nice to see your brain has returned."

"I *know* the Shepherd," I continued, ignoring his remark. "He would never plot against anyone."

I saw that peaceful look return to my brother's eyes. "So we can agree that Shepherd is our ally and the Wolf is our enemy?"

"Aye," I smiled. "And we can agree to avoid those dragon eggs as well."

"Without question," he affirmed with a stiff nod, and we began walking once again.

As we walked, I noticed he kept looking down at his sword,

admiring it with a slight look of awe on his face. As his hand moved in step at his side, I saw him tap his thumb to the sword, listen to it ring, and then quietly laugh to himself. This happened a few times before I felt obliged to say something.

"Are you off your head, mate?"

"So what about these swords, eh?" he answered.

"Indeed," I asked curiously, "what about them?"

"Remember that old claymore Da had hanging all those years above the fireplace?"

"Supposedly handed down through the clans and all that- from The Bruce-"

"Aye."

"Pretty sure that's bollocks."

"Aye, but that's not my point. What I'm trying to say is that, as lads, we both handled the claymore. You remember?"

"Aye. Secretly, against Da's wishes."

"An amazing piece of steel, that."

"It was hard to keep our hands off."

"Indeed," Drostan continued, "and these swords we're carrying: every bit as good, or better even, wouldn't you agree?"

"Aye, likely" I agreed with little thought, failing to see the point of the conversation.

"It's just got me to thinking... Shepherd's words are like a seed."

I was confused by the statement, and its disconnection to the conversation. "What are you on about?"

"I mean, think about your Rubber Plant seed. One little seed that was used to produce a whole bunch of things."

"...Alright...?"

"I'm just saying- it's like, everything about the Kingdom comes down to seeds. Shepherd spoke to the ground and his garden grew: *life*. Shepherd spoke to the rocks and the outer wall was erected: *protection*. Shepherd spoke to the Ergon and this sword was made," he held it up, "*a weapon*. And we both agree that this weapon is *effective*."

I looked at my brother with a shrug, "I've still no idea what you're trying to say to me, Dros."

"I'm not entirely sure either," he admitted, "except that these swords have some magical power even more than what we have the capacity to realize or understand. They're like our own, personal, physical embodiment of the Shepherd's magic."

"Truly fascinating, that," I widened my eyes in sarcasm. "Now can we just get along to the next terror that awaits us?"

I saw a genuine look of disappointment on his face, as his voice became slightly more somber, "You fail to see the importance of what I'm saying. I hope in time it comes to you."

It was about then that we noticed the black cloud. It must have been higher in the sky and descended, because we hadn't noticed it until it was merely a few feet from our heads. It appeared to be still descending, settling like a fog; and once it did surround us, we felt it on our bodies, like a weight.

I couldn't see anything. I put my hand to my face and I

couldn't even see it.

"What's happening?" asked Drostan in a muffled tone that startled me. The fog was so heavy it'd even impaired my hearing.

"It's just a fog, Dros," I called back, attempting to trivialize it.

"No it's not. I can *feel* it."

I couldn't lie to myself; I agreed with him, and I was worried.

"What do we do? We can't move forward if we can't see where forward is."

"I suppose we wait for it to lift," I answered.

"What if it doesn't? This is no ordinary fog."

"…Seems like one thing after another, doesn't it?"

"Aye. Bloody Snow Beasts and Tree Sprites, Diggers and dragon eggs…"

By this time, I had sat on the ground, and I could hear that Drostan had done the same.

"What if the Shepherd was wrong about us?" I finally asked.

"What do you mean?"

"I mean, don't get me wrong, I believe in the Shepherd. But, he sent us out as warriors because *he* believed in *us*."

"-And what if we're just two mates from Golspie?"

"-Exactly."

"Aye, I was just thinking the same thing. We've grown up tending sheep, mending fences, and playing football. What do we know about courage and honor and all that…?"

And at that very instant, it hit me like a ton of bricks; the understanding of what Drostan was trying to tell me earlier.

"Wait," I said. "Stop this."

"…What?"

"Stop this, *both* of us. You said we don't know about courage and honor, and I was about to agree with you, but you're wrong. We learned all there is to know about honor from growing up with a man like Da."

"…A good man, he was."

"-Indeed, an *honorable* man. And as for courage, we have it each right here at our side," and I reached down to ring the blade of my sword with my thumb.

"Well, I suppose you might have a point."

"-Nah, keep your '*suppose*.' There's no *maybe* to it. You were right, what you said earlier about these swords. I just couldn't get it at the time. Shepherd made these blades with a *word*, and there is *indeed* a powerful magic to his words, you said that yourself. What greater means of courage could we find anywhere, than to carry at our side the same magical power by which this whole Kingdom was made in the first place?"

For a moment there was silence, not a word between us.

"You're absolutely right, brother," he said with the resolve of newfound revelation, and I heard him stand with the quiet clink of his sword. I stood as well, and as mysteriously as it had come, the fog slowly lifted, and I saw the same violent passion in my brother's eyes that swelled in my own chest.

Drostan turned to me with that same look as when we first set off from the garden, that *Rangers vs. Manchester* grin. "If Shepherd believes in us, then we *are* the very warriors he's sent us out to be. Let's hunt dragon."

Chapter Sixteen

With the permanent smoke hovering overhead, it had felt like nighttime ever since we'd entered the Kingdom from the Back Meadow, which made our travel across the blackened plane of the once shimmering city feel all the more serious. We kept our minds to our purpose, without a word between us for the longest time, as we marched ever forward, focused on the battle before us.

Moving in, ever deeper toward the center of the Kingdom, the foul stench we'd smelled when we first arrived had gotten worse and worse. Now that we'd gotten close enough, we could see through the smoke to see where the foul stench was coming from; it was the black mote Tommy had told us about. Drostan and I both leaned over it to look in, and he began to quietly sing.

"I've sailed the wild Atlantic, crossed the broad Pacific shore, I've sailed around the stormy capes and I've heard the-"

"Are you serious?!" I interrupted angrily.

My brother startled with a look to me, surprised at the quick change of atmosphere. "...Well I realize this water isn't a *true* blue, but I just thought-"

"Are you seriously trying to-?" I stammered, just next to fury.

"How can you make jokes at a time like this?!"

He was silent for a moment to adjust to my seriousness.

He finally spoke, "Should I not? And why? Sometimes our wit is all we have, Branan."

We were silent for a moment before he continued.

"For most of our journey, you've been tense and worried, but has it helped you along? I think not-"

"Worry or no, I just don't see the need to make a bloody joke every thirty seconds in the middle of trying to save people's lives, especially after we've already lost one."

"Do you mean Jack?"

"Who else?"

He paused for a long moment. "Well, I truly do apologize if my sense of humor has offended you, mate, but I don't take his passing lightly. I just don't think he'd want you to continue focusing on it. Understand, I'd only once met the man, but he didn't seem to me to be the type to want everyone to mope around once he'd gone, but rather to keep smiling, making jokes, living... I don't know; it seems to me that *that* would honor him more."

I took into consideration all he'd said, and realized that my brother was right.

"You're right, brother," I finally said, with a humble smile. "If he was here, he'd have thought that was funny."

"Agreed. I *am* a rather witty human being, after all-" Drostan quickly changed the subject, leaning away from the mote. "Man, that's rank!"

"Indeed. And how are we going to get across it? We can't jump; it's too wide."

"And any one of these huge rocks would be far too heavy to move for a bridge."

"I suppose we'll have to swim."

"Might as well get it over with," he said, and then he secured his belt and jumped in. I followed him in before I had a chance to talk myself out of it.

The mucky goop was so thick that we fought to get through it, choking all the while on more horrid a stench than I've ever smelled before or since. The air was thick with it, like breathing neeps and tatties strait into your windpipe, but without the benefit of happy taste buds. I even swallowed some of it in the struggle, and it was truly unbearable. Worse than milk gone bad, or meat left out to spoil, it gagged me to breathlessness, but even worse than the taste was the feeling in my gut. It was like I had swallowed a pitcher full of death itself. It turned my stomach to rot, and I felt the very essence of decay in my body. I fought with everything in me to keep focused on the opposite bank and keep moving forward through the mote.

When we finally climbed out on the other side, we both succumbed to vomiting over and over, unable to get the stink out of our nostrils. We rolled ourselves in the ash of the ground frantically, hoping that it might sop up some of the stench that we each were wearing. It didn't help all that much, but eventually my nose just went numb to it, and Drostan said the same had happened to him. So we moved on.

As we continued on, the more ash there was, thick on the ground, in the air, almost *raining*, as it were. We saw more and more ash-covered rocks; huge, jagged rocks they were; they seemed to get bigger the further in we went. We figured we could use this to our advantage, and so we wove between them on our hands and knees, like traveling through a maze, careful to not let our swords ring off them in the jostle. If we could be quiet enough, we supposed, we may be able to come upon the Dragon unseen.

Drostan was in the lead, and I followed a couple feet or so behind. We kept hearing, several times as we crawled, a sort of puffing, popping sound. It was like the in-taking of a bellows, or the backfiring of a furnace, and it sounded surprisingly close.

Drostan wedged around between the rocks and leaned in close to me, almost touching his face against mine, so he could whisper as quietly as possible.

"Up there," he whispered.

My eyes followed up where he nodded and I saw the tops of huge, black boulders, what looked almost like the top of a natural stone wall. Something big, I couldn't tell what, was moving in the middle, up and down. I rubbed my eyes, squinting, looking harder through the black fumes. It was the Dragon, encircled by his ring of boulders, the wall he'd put in place from the clefts of the Distant Mountains.

We heard another furnace sound.

"I'm assuming those sounds are him sleeping," Drostan

whispered. "If so, here's what I want to do..."

I'll admit, I was scared. With that said, I was glad he'd taken initiative.

"First," he continued, "I'll go round this way," he motioned to a narrow path between rocks to our side. "Then, you make sure you're well hidden behind that boulder," he motioned to the huge, black rock the Dragon slept facing, "and drop whatever chunks and stones you can gather down onto his muzzle. But *don't start* dropping until you see me catch light off my blade. That'll be the sign that I'm ready; I don't want him waking up until I'm ready. Then, while he's distracted by your rocks, I'll crouch in behind him and open his belly with my sword."

"Right," I agreed to his plan.

"Good hunting," he said with a grin, before he went his way.

I climbed the rock wall, as quietly as possible, to crouch on the cleft just behind the boulder where I was to position myself, and looked around my feet for stones and rubbish.

I took a deep breath in, trying to get as much real air as possible amidst the toxic fumes, and thought of Shepherd, how he'd trusted us with this quest. I tried to focus on this thought to conjure up the courage I needed to continue.

I gathered up the stone rubbish and slowly moved to get into position to see around the boulders and the Dragon, so to see the glint I awaited from Drostan's blade. But as I did this, I hesitated just enough to lose footing, and I slid down the cleft and onto the next one, landing just in front of the boulder I was supposed to stand behind.

The noise I caused was a bit more than I thought necessary for a fall of so small a magnitude, and the beast awoke.

His eyes shot open right to me, just as his nostrils flared, expelling two identical coils of thick, black smoke.

My mind raced, and I considered that I had ruined the plan and that all was for naught; until I realized that I had actually *accomplished* the plan, just differently then planned. I had the Dragon's undivided attention.

Now all I had to do was not die.

I took my brother's idea and held up my sword, trying to find the sun with it. Once I discovered it peeking in behind the black clouds of smoke, I used my sword to reflect into the Dragon's eyes what little light it shone. Just then, I saw my brother creeping up slowly on the Dragon's flanks, sword raised high.

Just as he prepared to strike, to thrust his sword into the Dragon's underbelly, Drostan lost footing atop a patch of pebbles. His sword clanged against the stone as his chest hit the ground.

The Dragon didn't even bother to turn and see from where the noise had come. He just thrust forward to slam me back into the huge rock behind me, whipping his tail as he went. The massive, scaly tail caught Drostan up into the air with chunks of boulder, before slamming him back down beneath the huge, jagged rocks.

"Dros!" I yelled in a panic. I couldn't do anything to help him with the Dragon standing between us.

"I'm alright, brother!" he called back to me. "Might've broken my leg, but I'm not dying or nothing... But I'm pinned beneath the rocks..." he gasped for the air to speak, the wind knocked out of him, "Sorry mate, looks like you're on your own."

My thoughts raced as I considered my predicament.

What could I do? The Dragon had pinned me against the boulder, an immovable wall. Sure, my sword was drawn, but it was little more than a nuisance to my arm, which was pinned against the scales of the beast; my elbow the only thing between my face and that of the Dragon. And my other arm was pressed hard between my back and the rocks.

...I thought about Da, lying in bed back home, probably wondering where his boys were. I thought of Drostan, trapped and at the mercy of whatever would take place in the next few minutes. I thought of Jack, whose life had already been extinguished, and whose son and daughter faced the same fate if I couldn't win the day.

Ah, Cassia... I *had* to make it back to her...

And then it struck me like inspiration: leverage; I was *myself* the fulcrum I needed, between my two arms. Using this, the only leverage I had to my disposal, I braced the arm behind me firm against the rocks and forced my other elbow up with all my strength against the Dragon's chin.

His forked tongue whipped out, nearly catching me in the face with its poison. I heard a hiss from deep in his throat, followed by a rumbling even deeper in his bowels; that dreadful sound that preceded the furious, scorching flames.

With a newly discovered courage, I looked up into his hateful, black eyes.

"The Kingdom has no place for a dragon," I whispered to him in fury.

Then, gripping my fist tight around the hilt of my sword, I forced my elbow up just a bit more, stretching his neck into the wee spot of open space between us, and slid my blade through his throat.

Epilogue

"And that, my wee lass," my father said, giving a little self-approving nod at successfully finishing his story, "is how your uncle and I won back the Kingdom."

"So then what? Did you and Mom go back to stay in the Shepherd's Garden?"

"Aye."

"And Uncle Drostan and Aunt Crystal?"

"Aye, as well as your uncle Tommy; and from then on, all seemed to fit into place. Your ma and I were glad we'd given the football club to Tommy, and now that he was spending more and more time with the Shepherd, he was learning how to better manage such an establishment. Not to mention all the support the Shepherd provided; he stood behind the club, understand; said that 'such a community is very noble an accommodation to the Kingdom.' After awhile, Leather Leaf became quite a respectable association, so much so that Dros and I joined, forming the Williams Brothers Football Club."

"-That picture in the hall?" I interrupted, disbelieving.

"Aye, the only photograph we ever had taken."

"-That was in Dundee," I argued with a laugh. "The Riverside Bears."

"What?" Dad played innocent.

"Mom told me a long time ago that you and Uncle Dros played rugby on a small community team called the Riverside Bears."

My dad scratched his head, pretending confusion. "So I never played football for Leather Leaf?"

I laughed.

"I'm starting to wonder," he said, still scratching his head, "maybe you should tell the stories from now on. I'm getting the facts all wrong, looks like…"

"So, what about you and Mom?"

"Hm?"

"You never finished that part of the story."

"Ah yes," he feigned remembrance, "I nearly forgot. As for your ma and I, we asked the Shepherd for a wee spot near the meadow and we planted our seeds side by side. Just like your uncle Drostan and his Crystal, our seeds sprouted and grew up to entwine together."

"What was it?"

"It grew into a tiny, precious sapling that quickly became a beautiful tree. It bore fruit and made us proud."

"…It didn't become a cocoon or a meadow or anything?"

"Nope. Your ma and I didn't need anything like that. We were proud enough of our little tree just to be our tree. And we named our tree Patricia."

I smiled as he touched my nose with a wink, "And she's made us proud every day since."

...Since I was that little girl, tucked in bed listening to my dad, not so incredibly much has changed about the world really. I mean, sure times change a bit, but people are pretty much the same as things cycle back around; they make both good and bad decisions, hoping to be remembered for the good ones. And through the years, though I've made my share of bad decisions, I think I might just be remembered for the good ones.

We only have the ability to make good decisions by having taken that ability from what we've learned here or there. Only now, raising my own daughter, can I look back and see how much I've really taken from my Daddy's story.

The End

Appendix I: The Beautiful Game

Welcome to the Leather Leaf Football Club! For most of you, having spent your whole life here in the Kingdom and therefore knowing little about things outside; as well as others of you who have come from some sad land where football is not commonly played, I've decided to provide this exposition as a brief history of Football, as well as a brief history of Leather Leaf.

As to Football, it likely originated a very long time ago in a place called Greece. However, the current and most widely celebrated form of football, Association Football (sometimes called Soccer), began in England, and is governed largely by a rule code called the Cambridge Rules, and the subsequent rule codes thereafter.

After Football's formation, time passed, meetings took place, committees were formed, dissolved, and reformed, and eventually, The Football Association (FA) was formed. After several meetings in London, The FA, because of a disagreement concerning the game rule code, divided into two separate entities: The Football Association and the Rugby Football Union.

Nearly a decade later, four clubs; The Football Association, the Scottish Football Association, the Football Association of Whales, and the Irish Football Association sat to a meeting in Manchester, and the International Football Association Board (IFAB) was founded. The laws of the current game of Football are determined by IFAB.

The first official international football game was between Scotland and England and took place in Glasgow. The game, watched by four thousand spectators, was a draw. Since this first game in Scotland, the game of Football has become a passion to people from everywhere. It is so loved, that the phrase "The Beautiful Game," coined by a Brazilian footballer named Didi, became its nickname.

As concerns Football here in the Kingdom, the Leather Leaf Football Club was the first and is the only football association to date. It was founded by Branan Williams and Cassia Ross. Although *Club* is in the title, Leather Leaf is more appropriately understood as an association, as it is the Kingdom's only organized Football venue, and many teams belong to it.

In the first year of its existence, Leather Leaf grew from a humble footballer's shop to a club of training clinics and ten competing teams. Its single playing field with handcrafted goals and bleachers hosted 67 games, before the field and all surrounding land was destroyed. The following year, the club was rebuilt, the new field grown up atop the ashes of the old.

Since its rebuilding, Leather Leaf now boasts 24 teams: The Williams Brothers, Cane Grove Kickers, The Oakmen, Jaron's Clan, The Ivy Road Eleven, Team Wallace, Madelyn's Mates, Moss Avenue Millers, Spring Mountain Trackers, Team McCulloch, The

Stone-Crafters Guild, Pine Grove Loggers, The Hedgeway Hawks, Freddy's Fighters, Team Ross, Cedar Lane Stompers, The Shepherd's Eleven, Silverking, The Plowmen, The Willow Tree, Team McLaren, William's Wallop, Boys of Bluefern, and Team Willis.

As a new member of Leather Leaf, you are encouraged to join one of these clubs, though the starting of a new club, once having received the authority from the Leather Leaf Club Manager to do so, is not forbidden.

Also, as a member of Leather Leaf, you are encouraged to research Football history, a task that is quite well accommodated now as the Shepherd has graciously added a new Football department to the Kingdom Library on *Bluefern Lane*. Reading about important games of the past, styles of play, and even specific team histories can benefit a player by helping him to see the Game objectively.

It is also encouraged, once a member has become somewhat educated, to choose a favorite non-Kingdom team to support, and follow that club exclusively, as per season records and individual player statistics.

As Leather Leaf is a fundamentally Scottish founded club, the managerial staff encourages members to become educated in the history of the Old Firm. It is not mandated that a member be a supporter of the Rangers, the Celtic, or even of the Old Firm collectively; it is however advised.

None of the managerial staff would attempt to impose upon

any member of Leather Leaf any particular allegiance or abhorrence, though being a supporter of Manchester United is of course frowned upon.

Often times, good-natured rivalries between supporters carry over onto the playing field and can become less than good-natured. In regard to these and any other reasons, every Leather Leaf footballer is hereby warned that no fighting will be tolerated. One incident will result in a suspension for three games; a second incident will result in the expulsion from Leather Leaf.

Every member of this football club is encouraged to keep in mind that the purpose of the club is friendly competition and community. And as a healthy community of footballers, we are glad you have chosen to become a part of our community. Once again, welcome to Leather Leaf!

Manager Tommy Ross

Appendix II: The Shepherd's Story

I had a bride once. She was all I ever wanted in a bride. She loved and trusted me unconditionally, and I loved her the same. We would walk in my garden for hours and hours, just to talk about whatever came into conversation. And in time, we brought children into the world, and loved them with the same unconditional love with which we loved each other. Raising our children in the garden, it was all they knew, and they were happy.

But as time passed, my bride became distracted. She became more interested in the many wares of my garden than she was in spending time walking with me. As I walked alone in my garden, I would see her far off, preoccupied with this or that, very little thought ever of me.

Children, at least when they are young, usually relate more with and feel more comfortable around their mother than their father. There is usually a calmer way about a mother that a child is endeared to. That's just the way it is. Because of this natural way of things, my sons and daughters seemed to relate to my bride more than to me.

Though I was pleased to see the bonds forming between my children and my bride, it made me sad to see them from far off, knowing that the family I loved was growing apart from me.

The years passed, and when my children had grown, the relationship between us had grown from love to fear. They acknowledged who I was, that I was their father, but had very little interest in walking with me or talking with me. My bride had all but forgotten me, or at least it seemed. I figured she must have spent so much time away from me that she had forgotten my true nature, or else why would she have taught our children to fear me?

I called out to my bride, but she wouldn't hear. I would come to her in the morning and ask her to walk with me like we had done so often in times past, but she ignored me. I didn't understand it, but I loved her still, just as much as in the beginning, and would not force her to walk with me if she didn't want to. So I still came to her and called out her name, but less often and less loudly, to give her the space she wanted.

By the time my grandchildren were born into the garden, they grew up never even knowing my name. I pleaded with my bride to teach the truth about me to our children and grandchildren, but she still seemed to ignore me. I don't think she even recognized my voice anymore.

She brought our grandchildren into a house she had created. I noticed that my name had been written above the door, and my heart was revived. Now, I thought, maybe my bride will teach my family how I love them. Maybe they will learn my name and call out to me to come and walk with them.

And so I entered the house my bride had built with pleasure to see that it was full of my children and grandchildren. I walked right into the middle of them and was shocked to realize that they didn't even notice me. They were all looking forward, where my bride was standing, reciting loudly that which they repeated unanimously line for line. She was reading a long list of things not to say, things not to do, so as to not make me angry.

I spoke up, explaining that these weren't the important things. Not a list of avoidances, but to truly know me, *that* was what mattered. I began explaining how I loved them all, and that I didn't want them to be afraid of me, but that I wanted to know them. Sadly, it was then that I realized I was talking to myself; none of them were listening. They were all deaf to me, listening intently to the words of my bride, who seemed also to be completely oblivious to me.

Not knowing what else I might try to get her attention, I left her house.

As the years passed, my bride took my children further and further from me, all the while, convincing herself that she was doing right by me, teaching them what she called my ways. Once my grandchildren had come of age to have children of their own, there was a sea of faces bearing my likeness, but my name had become a curse word to them. In all this time, somehow love had become fear and fear had become hatred.

The grandchildren of my children hated me, for reasons they themselves didn't even understand. They hated my bride as well, for my name above the door of the house she had built. I found it quite strange that, though my bride no longer knew me, she was hated for my sake.

I was sad for her, to see her far off and all alone. Very few of our children still came to the house she had built. The few who came took up the same monotonous recitation as had echoed off the walls of the house since its creation, never a thought of me, the father it poorly represented.

Finally, after so long a time, I decided it was time I act. Early one morning, I wielded a sledge and destroyed the house of my bride. Into little tiny bits I beat it, dismembering it to dust and rubble, and I stood atop the heap.

When my bride came to gather with my children, they were aghast to see it destroyed. My children were still blind to me, seeing only the remains of their meetinghouse, but my bride saw me. With her empire reduced to rubble, she was forced to remember my face, and recognize that it was I who stood before her.

I'd of course hoped that this would unite her to me once again, that we could finally raise our children together. But she was far from endeared to me. In fury, she hurled her accusations at me.

"What kind of father," she screamed, "would destroy the house of his children?"

I knew then that it was lost, all chance of us being reconciled. She had convinced herself of what was to be, and the truth would not dissuade her. Sadly, I decided that if I were to know any of my children, whom I could not stand to live without, I must turn my back on the bride I loved.

Suddenly then, just as I turned to walk away, I felt a little hand slip into mine. I looked down to see a bright, inquisitive face I could never have expected to see. She must have been the smallest, the youngest of my children. She looked into my face, and her little voice quivered as she spoke my name.

Finally! I had found one who still knew me!

I embraced her in my arms and she laughed as I spun her around.

"You are my heritage," I told her, "and together we will build a house of our own."

Appendix III: Adopted Sisters
(Note from the Author)

I grew up with three brothers. I was the third. And although many things about coming of age in a house full of boys was awesome, I'd always kind of wished I had a sister. So somewhere around probably 1990 or so, at Bear Lake summer camp in north-central Indiana, when I met a girl named Rachael Drye, I sort of "adopted" her as my sister. Come to find out, our fathers (both of whom were pastors) were friends. Rachael was, almost immediately, someone who felt like family to me, and since I'd always wished I had a sister, it happened kind of naturally. She'll always be special to me and we're still like family all these years later.

About 10 or 11 years after meeting Rachael, a few years before Abigail Staker (of Miami County, Indiana) became my sister-in-law (in that she and my brother Kevin were married), I sort of "adopted" her as a sister as well. Then, a similar thing happened around 2006, when I met a girl named Kallie Engle (of Southeastern Oklahoma), who later also, like Abby, became my sister-in-law (in that she and my brother-in-law Micah were married), and so I had yet *another* chosen sister.

All that said to say that these things of course seemed very coincidental, but appear to me to be very *providential*, in that I chose to be connected to someone who then later became literally connected, in important ways, to my life.

In like manner, between Abigail and Kallie, I also "adopted" Toni Robbins and Cassia and Trish Key (all three of Arlington, Texas); the first of whom with which I share a last name and no common genetics, the second and third of whom are much of the basis of two primary characters in this book.

Thanks for reading, and may the Original Self be your only source.
-A.C. Robbins

Made in the USA
Middletown, DE
04 October 2023